*a
novel
by*

J Russell Rose

ISBN: *978-1-4357-5339-6*
Publisher: *Lulu.com*
Rights Owner: *J Russell Rose*
Copyright: © 2007 *Standard Copyright License*

ALSO BY

J Russell Rose

Looking Down on the Moon

In Search of Himself

Murder in Pleasant Grove

Marilee

READER REACTION: *Many of the novels by J Russell Rose take the reader on a journey. MISSING follows that pattern. If you are an arm chair traveler come along for a ride, I think you will enjoy it immensely.*

MISSING addresses the worldwide problem of people who simply vanish. Through one man's brutal abduction, and another's determination to find him, the writer gives a view into the workings of the various Missing Persons units.

More than one hundred thousand Americans' names populate the FBI's Missing Persons files. Many of those people, sadly will never be found.

MISSING is the story of one such missing person – Tim Addison. It is also the story of the determination of his brother Mark and dedicated Richmond, VA, police officer Mary O'Brien, to find him.

MISSING will keep you glued to the pages from start to finish.

To Awa
Thank you!
J Russell Rose
8-03-2013

PART ONE

Mark Addison knew something was dreadfully wrong. There had to be a reason why they had not heard from his brother Tim in the more than three weeks since he left on a trip to New Mexico and Colorado for some hiking and fishing. It wasn't like Tim to break off communication with his family. He was the one who called every week, at least, just to "keep in touch."

Tim had always been, though on the surface he seemed introspective and reserved, the adventurous one of the three brothers. Mark and Eric the more serious, both studied medicine at the Medical College. Eric was now an orthodontist, who had made a small fortune improving the smiles of wealthy Richmondites' children, and Mark had a successful general private practice; originally his dad's practice, down in the Fan District, before university expansion took the building. His patients were mostly elderly who had stuck with their old (some rather large and stately) homes on and around Monument and Grove Avenues.

He sat, worried and contemplative that morning, staring out the window of his office at the slow-moving traffic on Patterson Avenue, an area which used to be considered the far west end of Richmond. Now the West End seemed to stretch halfway to Charlottesville on either side of I-64.

Mark smiled as his thoughts momentarily switched to one of his patients, Mrs. Green. Hilda Mary Green, age eighty-seven, she announced herself to the receptionist, who complained to him, on each visit, about the way everyone was abandoning the city for the suburban counties. "Why my niece just bought a house way out in Hanover. 'Why on earth do you want to go that far from the city and the shopping,' I asked her? Why the buses don't even run out there. How will I ever get to visit you?"

But Hilda Green was not coming in to Dr. Mark's office today. No one was. He had canceled all his appointments for the rest of the week, intent on making some sense of this thing with Tim. He couldn't do that with a full patient load. He knew he would catch a lot of grief from the ones who were being canceled and rescheduled. Mrs. Green, Mr. Day, Mr. Turner, Mrs. Gates, and Mrs. Katz, and all the others were going to be furious.

"Why I made this appointment over two months ago," Mrs. Katz protested. "I need my medicines refilled. I can't wait another two months."

Ginny, the new receptionist, one of the best Mark had ever had, could be heard apologizing, "I'm sorry, Mrs. Katz. The Doctor has an emergency. We will be happy to call your pharmacist about your medicines. Can you come in at nine forty-five on the twenty-second?" A pause for more protest, then she said, "Thanks a lot Mrs. Katz. We'll see you then."

He was probably just over reacting, but something inside told him that there was indeed a problem. Not being a detective, though, he really didn't know where to begin. His brother Eric had suggested they contact the family attorney and ask for help in getting credit card and bank transaction records. They were going to meet at Tim's apartment later today, looking for what, they weren't sure, but it was a place to start.

TWO

Tim Addison, the thirty-three year old sibling of Mark and Eric, was more like a son than a brother. Together they supported him financially as well as emotionally. "It's time you grew up Timmy," they would lecture him, either jointly or separately, each time he had another money "emergency."

Tim took their lectures and chiding in stride for the most part. However, nothing seemed to work; and now, this. Each of the brothers was thinking that had they been tougher on Tim, forcing him to take charge and do something, this would not, could not, have happened.

After the death of their parents, both within the past ten years, first their mother then their dad, Tim seemed to loose his newly found mooring, along with what resolve and drive he had built up. He had grown up in the house alone. Both Mark and Eric were gone soon after he was born – a menopausal accident. Their dad had jokingly said, "It was one last effort at youth and immortality."

Tim had lived in the house with his parents, except for several seasons in Colorado, until they died – then he didn't want to stay there any longer. Mark and Eric were both a little apprehensive, when Tim announced he was leaving for this trip to New Mexico and Colorado.

Who are you going with," they wanted to know?

"When are you coming back? Do you have money? Is this a safe venture?"

"You two sound little a couple of old hens," was Tim's comment.

Then he added, "I'm a big boy now, in case you hadn't noticed."

Mark arrived at the apartment just minutes after his brother. As they went into the building, both feeling rather like felons about to burglarize the place, they nervously looked around to see if they were being watched.

"Relax, will you," Eric scolded. "You're making me nervous. We pay the rent on this joint, after all. I guess we have a right to be here."

There had allegedly been a parade of live-in girlfriends over the past few years, so just in case there was anyone there, they knocked first, then called, "Hello," as they entered.

"Will you look at this place? Where is the Health Department, when you need them?" Eric wanted to know.

"Good grief," Mark responded. "What a mess."

The apartment was strewn with empty and partially empty beer cans, pizza boxes, an assortment of discarded items of clothing, and other various elements of discord.

"How long since you've been here?" Mark asked his brother.

"I haven't. How about you?"

"I was here once, about six months back, I guess. Sure didn't look like this."

With a joint shaking of heads, they turned their attention to the pile of mail, which had accumulated inside the door beneath the mail slot, sorting through, looking for some clue as to Tim's whereabouts.

They found the usual junk mail assortment; one offering Timothy Addison a 2.9% APR, Credit Card. Another announced, "You may have already won a million dollars…"

There was really not much of significance to the novice sleuths.

"Here's a bank statement," Mark offered.

"Here are two overdraft notices from the same bank," Eric added. "He bounced a check for four dollars and fifty-one cents at a convenience store. Probably for beer, which is now going to cost him, correction us, about fifty bucks."

"Here is the VISA statement," Mark mentioned without response to the bad check notice.

"Let's have a look. That could be helpful."

"Nope. The last item is more than three weeks ago, prior to his leaving."

"Any letters from anyone in the Southwest?"

"Nothing."

"Well, Sherlock, what do we do now?"

Mark Addison walked to the window, deep in thought. "I think we should contact the police."

"And tell them exactly what?" his brother countered.

"Tell them what we know so far. Our brother, who is extremely reliable about keeping us informed of his whereabouts, has not made contact for more than three weeks."

"I suppose we really don't have any choice. Should we have someone clean up here?"

"Probably not. There could be some evidence we're missing."

"Good point."

"I have rescheduled all my appointments for the rest of the week. How about you?"

"I'll do that in the morning. I have a couple of early mornings tomorrow; I'll probably take care of them. I know someone at Police Headquarters who can probably direct us to the right person. I'll get hold of him then I'll call you around nine?"

"That sounds good."

They left the apartment together, driving off for home, each more concerned than he was willing to admit. Something was very wrong. They both knew it.

THREE

The brothers decided to meet at a local eatery on West Cary Street for lunch, prior to driving downtown to the main police station. Avoiding the subject that both had on their minds, they made small talk while eating.

"How's Marianne," Mark asked concerning Eric's wife.

"Fine. How about Patty?"

"Fine. The boys?"

"They're okay. How are Pam and Michelle?"

"Michelle has another new boy friend. I'm afraid to open the door sometimes to these characters. Patty says they're harmless. But they look rather disreputable as a lot. Sometimes I wish we'd had boys. I don't know if I'll survive being the father of girls."

"I'm sure it really isn't much easier with boys. I mean with drugs and sex, and drugs and sex, you have to tell them the right things. With girls you could just lock them up till they're twenty-one."

"If only it were that easy. By the way, what has Marianne had to say about this situation with Tim?" Mark decided it was time to stop avoiding the issue and talk about what they were going to do.

"Well, you know how Marianne feels about Tim."

"Yes. She certainly hasn't kept her feelings a secret."

"She thinks we're over reacting. That Tim has found some Babe in the mountains and has dropped out of sight because he has more pressing things to attend to."

"Frankly, I wish she were right. I mean, then when he did show up again, we could give him a good tongue-lashing about scaring the Hell out of us and get on with it."

"But, you really don't think that's the case, do you?"

"No. I'm afraid I don't."

"Me neither."

Having spoken to each other what they had not wanted to admit to themselves, seemed to help. Now they could talk openly about their worst fears, knowing the other felt the same.

"What time is our appointment at Police Headquarters?" Mark asked since his brother had made the contact.

"We're to meet a Sgt. O'Riley in the Missing Persons section at one-thirty."

"Guess we should be heading out then."

They paid their check at the register then returned to the parking lot where they had met earlier. Eric wasn't too keen about taking his new Mercedes downtown to the police station, so he suggested they take Mark's car, even though he really didn't like his brother's driving all that much.

They headed east till they picked up the expressway and entered the stream of traffic toward Downtown Richmond. Thanks to the miracles of modern highway engineering, a few minutes later, they arrived at their destination, a trip, which in the sixties and seventies could have taken them forty-five minutes to an hour to make.

Entering the nearly windowless, rather odd-looking structure, which at one time was a shining testimonial to modern architecture, and was now just another example of urban decay and neglect, they scanned the area for an information booth; a directory – anything that would guide them to the office they wanted. Spotting a young woman at a desk across the foyer, they approached, asking for the location of Missing Persons.

"Second floor. Take the elevator over there. Turn left upon exiting. Second door on your right," the woman responded in an automaton-like voice, without looking up and without responding to their, "Thank you."

The missing person's office was humming when they entered. Phones were demanding to be answered, as one uniformed person yelled, "Will someone please get the damn phone."

They stepped up to the front desk where another young woman sat, who without looking up, asked, "May I help you?"

"Sgt. O'Riley, please."

"Name?"

"Eric Addison."

"Take a seat. Someone will be with you shortly."

They sat down in the cheap molded plastic chairs by the door, looking around the room trying to take in the confusion and chaos. Each was wondering how anyone could get anything done in such an atmosphere.

"Dr. Addison?" the soft-voiced person seemed to quiet the room. "I'm Mary O'Riley."

More than a little confused, Eric replayed the conversation he had had the day before. He was certain he had spoken to a man – at least he knew this was not the voice on the phone.

"I'm sorry," he said, realizing the woman was holding out her hand while he was just staring at her. "I guess I was expecting... I mean... Did we speak on the phone?"

Eric realized he was babbling at this attractive young woman, when his brother spoke up.

"I'm Mark Addison," he said taking the woman's hand. "You'll have to forgive my brother. He seems to have taken leave of his senses."

"It's quite all right, I assure you. Would you gentlemen come with me?"

Eric trailed his brother obediently, embarrassed by the fact that he had lost his composure, something that rarely happened. They went into a dark, small partitioned windowless cubicle, which seemed airless to Mark. Mary O'Riley seated herself across the table from the two Doctors, Addison, smiling slightly at Eric's obvious discomfort. "What can I do for you?"

"Well," Mark Addison spoke up, "it seems our younger brother is missing."

"Why do you think your brother is missing?"

"We have not heard from him in three weeks, which is not normal."

"When did you last see your brother and what is his full name?"

"It was mid-week the second week of July."

"Timothy Alan Addison," Eric interjected somewhat abruptly, adding, "That's his full name."

"Do you know his date of birth?"

"February 27, 1966."

"Was he born in Richmond?"

"Yes," Mark answered.

"No," Eric corrected. "He was born in Henrico County."

"How tall is he and how much does he weigh?"

"Well, I'd say Tim is at least six-one, wouldn't you?"

"Yes," Eric added. "He would weigh no more than one-eighty, though. He's kind of skinny."

"What were the events of your last meeting? Did you have a fight or disagreement?"

"No," they both replied in unison.

Mark then continued. "We met Tim for lunch. He had called saying he wanted to get together with us since he was going on a trip."

"What was the purpose and destination of the trip?"

"Fishing," Eric responded. "He said he was going fishing and hiking,"

"In New Mexico, then he was going on to Colorado," Mark added.

Mary O'Riley was having a bit of trouble keeping up with the tag-team responses she was getting from the two of them, so she decided to tape the interview.

"If you don't mind," she stated, "I'd like to tape this conversation."

They did not, they both agreed.

"Now," she paused, after looking at what notes she had made and recording comments about them. "Did Tim seem upset or depressed at you meeting?"

"Quite the contrary, he seemed unusually optimistic."

"Why do you say, unusually?" she wanted to know. "Is he normally a depressed person?"

"Not really," Eric offered. "Do you think so?" he asked looking at Mark. "That would be more your area than mine. I just fix teeth."

"Well, I'm not a psychiatrist, just a GP" Mark stated. "But, I don't think he was, or is a depressed person. Tim has always been rather serious; kept to himself a lot as he was growing up. But I don't think you would say he was a depressed person. Though, I guess he had been a little down in the past few years since the death of our parents. He lived at home with them, you see."

"I see. How was he planning to travel?"

"He was driving."

"Can you give me a description and license number of the vehicle?"

"The vehicle is a '94 Ford Bronco. I would have to look for the license number. I don't know that we have it."

"We can get it from DMV. What color is the Bronco?"

"Green and silver, I guess you would call it? Mark?"

"I would."

"Do you have a recent photograph of your brother?"

Eric reached into the large envelope he was holding, now feeling unusually proud of himself for being prepared. As he handed the photo to Mary O'Riley, he said, "This is the most recent photo I could find."

Visibly shaken by the oddly handsome, long-haired young man, whose bearded face with the saddest brown eyes she had ever seen, stared back at her. Unknowingly, if unintentionally, she began hammering questions at the two brothers.

"How current is this picture?"

"It was probably taken last summer," Eric answered.

"Are the features – the hair and beard, especially, still the same?"

"Yes. At least they were, when we saw him at lunch."

"Although," Mark offered, "I think the hair and beard were shorter and more neatly trimmed."

"Does he any birthmarks? Scars? Tattoos?"

"None," both brothers agreed.

Unable to break the hold of those eyes in the photograph, wondering why they were affecting her so, Mary was quiet for a while.

Then with a slight shiver, she asked, "What can you tell me about Tim's lifestyle? Is he a party person? Does he drink heavily? Does he use drugs? Does he gamble? Is he familiar with the area he was to travel?"

The two brothers looked at each other realizing, with some degree of shock, that they really didn't know the answers to those questions.

"I don't think so. He's always seemed rather quiet, as I said," Mark offered sadly.

"Do you have any reason to believe he had unusual sexual preferences or habits?"

"If you're asking is he gay, I don't think so. He always had a lot of girl friends,"

Eric commented. "At least that was my impression."

"He spent two or three winters in Colorado a few years back. He worked as a ski instructor there. I don't know that he had ever been to New Mexico, though. He flew out to Denver on the earlier trips. This was his first time to drive there."

"How often did you see your brother prior to this trip?"

"We probably saw him once or twice a month, at least. And he usually called more frequently, 'Just to keep in touch,' as he put it."

"Were you very close to your brother, emotionally, I mean? Would he come to you with his problems?"

Eric chuckled, "Oh, yeah. We were the first to know when there was a problem. That is if money was involved."

"Where did your brother work?"

"I don't think he was working anywhere, currently," Mark stated.

"How did he support himself?"

Again the two brothers stared at each other with a touch of guilt in the look. Had they been firmer with Tim, again, they both thought, they might not be here.

Eric spoke up, somewhat hesitantly. "I guess you could say we supported him. Timmy is an unusual sort of person.

He's obviously gifted, but he lacked motivation and direction in his life. We really did try to help him with that, but nothing ever seemed to work. I guess we just finally concluded it was easier to just pay his bills than fight with him about it."

Hoping for some support, he looked at Mark, who added, "And, quite honestly, his lifestyle was by no means extravagant. His needs were simple. He was a jeans and Tee shirt guy."

"Well," Mary O'Riley said standing up from the desk, "I think I have everything I need from the two of you. First of all, I need to get this information on the wire and I will keep in touch with you. I think you should know that there are over one hundred thousand people in the FBI Missing Persons Computer Bank, with hundreds more added every week. Some people turn up in a few weeks, having just decided to go off on a lark or a whim without telling anyone. Hopefully, that is the situation with your brother. Others have been in the system for years with little or no progress made in finding them. The key to finding Tim, if he is indeed truly missing, is information – about his habits. His likes, his dislikes. I need a list of all his friends or acquaintances – old girlfriends, people who may have moved out west. Believe me, the more information you can give me, the better our chances of finding him. So, if you can think of anything else, anything at all, let me know."

"Thank you," Mark offered.

"Yes," Eric added. "Thank you for your time."

As the two men left the office, Mary O'Riley stared after them, hoping her gut feeling in this case was wrong and asking herself again, why the sad-eyed young man in the picture, at which she was again looking, had affected her so. Unfortunately she had seen this all before, all too often, in fact. A gifted, usually sensitive, young person of her generation, who was over-indulged by parents, or, as in this case older siblings; who was not allowed to fight his own life-battles; not allowed or forced, if necessary, to fend for himself, ending up a casualty of life in the "real world."

She shivered again as a fellow officer stuck his head in the door breaking her trance-like state, "Mary. There's a phone call for you."

"Thanks Ben," she said after a very long pause.

He started to walk away then noticing the strangely pale look on his colleague, he stepped into the room, "Mary? Are you all right?"

Ben Stewart, who was more than just a casual acquaintance of Mary O'Riley, closed the door and moved toward her. "Hey? What's going on?"

"I don't know," she responded truthfully, offering the photograph of Tim Addison to Ben.

"Who's this?" he asked becoming really worried about her.

"Another lost soul, I'm afraid," she responded, "one more, probable statistic for the log book. Sometimes," she paused and then tried again to voice what she was feeling. "Sometimes, I get so angry. Here is a person – a real human being of obvious intelligence and ability, who is treated like he is mentally deficient, by the people closest to him – the very ones who are supposed to prepare him for life in this world.

This is a thirty-three year old man who lived with his parents until their deaths. After that, he is supported by his two brothers out of some sort of misguided feelings of love and obligation. Now he's missing. And they don't have a clue as to why. Well just maybe he finally got tired of it all; the handouts; the demeaning looks; the asides and snickers. Just maybe he finally got the courage to stand on his own two feet and make a break for it and from them. Maybe he's out there somewhere, finally free from it all, free from them – even thumbing his nose at them, telling them all to go to Hell, and having the time of his life."

"You don't really think that's the case, though. Do you, Mary?"

"No. No, Ben, I don't. I got this sick feeling in the bottom of my gut when they handed me that photograph and I looked into those eyes. I thought to myself, 'Oh, God. This guy wouldn't survive a week on the mean streets of this country.' None of them had given him anything he needed; except money. It's always the same story. 'Here, take some money. Go buy yourself something. Be a good kid now. We have our own lives to live. We don't have time to help you with your problems. You need more? No problem. Run along, now."

"Aren't you being a little harsh on these people? Maybe, even presumptive?"

"Presumptive? The good brothers, both respected medical men, pillars of the community, didn't know if their missing brother had ever been on drugs; if he had a drinking problem; if he gambled; if he was gay. All they knew was it was easier to 'pay his bills than to fight about it.' Because his needs were few. His lifestyle was simple.'"

She tossed the photo on top of the notes which would eventually be transcribed and entered into the *Official File* of ***Timothy Alan Addison, MP*** (missing person). She found herself unable to breathe as she left the room for the telephone, wondering what the next crisis would bring.

FOUR

Mary O'Riley graduated in the top ten percent of her class at the University of Virginia, with a double major in Criminal Justice and Psychology. Recruited, prior to graduation, by the City of Richmond Police Department for a job in criminal investigations, she came to Missing Persons five years ago.

She was good at what she did. The only criticism her superiors had ever made of her was, "Mary gets too involved in her cases."

How could you not get involved, she wanted, no, she demanded to know. When she had been in the job long enough not to be moved by the story of a run-away teen or an abducted child, she knew it would be time to leave the department.

The oldest of three, hers was a typical working-class Richmond family. Her father worked at Reynolds Metals and her mother, who had briefly taught elementary school, seemed contented to be a full time at-home mom and wife for her family.

They lived in Lakeside, a quiet older Richmond neighborhood, of modest one story brick homes, with well manicured lawns and typical unpretentious landscaping – azaleas being the predominating choice of the area homeowners. The O'Riley's yard was similar, but also included an iris garden and gazebo, one of her father's many woodworking projects.

Mary and her two sisters were all good students, active in extra-curricular activities. Mary was the true over-achiever of the family. She was captain of the debate team, which took competition honors each year she was there; president of the student government; class officer two out of three years; also active in drama and choir. She became Valedictorian of her graduating class at Hermitage High School, and unlike most of her classmates, knew exactly what she wanted to do and study after graduation – Criminal Justice, at the University of Virginia.

"Why?" her father asked, genuinely perplexed. "Mary. Kitten. You could be anything you want to be. Why not study law – become an attorney?"

"But this is exactly what I want to do, Dad. I want to help people. I don't want to worry about keeping my fat-cat clients out of jail so they can help me pay for my new Jag or Porsche."

"Why not medicine? You could certainly help people there, too."

"You just don't get it, do you Dad? I don't want to be rich, at least not because of other people's misfortunes or illness. I want to make a difference. I want to help the people that no one else cares about. I should probably become a revolutionary."

Choosing to ignore that last remark, which he felt certain was intended just to annoy or irritate him, he made one last feeble plea for reason to prevail. "You'll be underpaid, overworked and under-appreciated. Is that what you want?"

"There are worse things. This is my life, my future, my dream. This is what I want to do."

With that statement, William O'Riley knew that was the end of the discussion. He had always tried to instill confidence in his daughters. He wondered if his efforts had been too much, or had backfired.

Mary studied hard at the University. She had no time for, or interest in Sororities or social clubs. She was, however, tireless in her work with causes that affected women, children, minorities and other disenfranchised peoples. She wrote countless letters to Congressmen and other elected officials in which she decried the continued mistreatment of Native Americans. She deplored the ethnic cleansing campaigns in Africa and the Balkan region, as well as the displacement of other individuals around the world.

One protest letter she wrote to the First Lady was so compelling that she was invited to the White House. She wrote: "... *I find it unconscionable for so many to remain silent regarding the plight of the illegal immigrant, who comes to this country hoping for nothing more than just a chance (the very basis for the founding of this great nation); not a handout, but, just possibly, a helping hand; for just a taste of the sweet nectar flowing in this land of milk and honey - which we, mostly, take for granted as our birthright. When, merely, that portion of what we have and produce that is simply wasted – thrown away every day, could make such a difference to one who has so little or nothing at all; I repeat. It is unconscionable to remain silent...*"

The meeting attendees were dubbed, "College Students with Causes". She came away from the meeting sorely disappointed, realizing it was just a pseudo "pat-on-the-back" and photo opportunity for the First Lady and other incumbent politicians, rather than a forum for discussion and interchange of ideas.

On her trip back to Charlottesville, looking at the certificate she had been given, Mary realized with considerable disappointment, that she didn't want any congratulatory recognition. She wanted to make a difference – she wanted to change things. Or, at the very least, she wanted someone to explain to her why these things had to be the way they were. Why these inequities had to exist. Sadly, she realized no one seemed to have the answers or solutions. And most people in power seemed all too often to simply not give a damn.

In the field of Criminal Justice, she hoped – prayed, to be of aid and assistance to battered and abused women and children. She struggled in the Domestic Relations unit for two years trying to find ways to get around bureaucracy and department "Red-tape" so she could really help those who could not help themselves, with only slight achievements.

Entering her third year with the department, an opening became available in the Missing Person's Unit, a position which she neither sought nor, at first, even wanted. However, the head of the unit, a very persuasive individual, convinced her that there was much good that could be done in the area of runaways, abductions, and the like. She made the move and had not looked back.

In Missing Persons', unlike Domestic Relations, she was given the leeway to do her job. She had a direct link to the information files of the FBI as well as many private funded search organizations. However, she never considered that the job would become her life.

"When do you have fun?" a well-meaning coworker had asked.

"I'm not sure I remember how," she responded with way too much seriousness in her voice.

She had dated Ben Stewart, a divorced father of two little girls, for about a year and a half, during which time. He had been pressing her for a commitment of some sort, almost one time too many.

"Mary, I love you," he told her, almost in tears of desperation the previous Christmas. "My girls love you. We want you to be a permanent part of our lives."

"Ben. I love you, too, and the girls feel like my own."

"So, what's the problem here? Why can't we become a family?"

"I don't know. I'm just not ready. My job takes up far too much of my time. I'm afraid I wouldn't have enough left over to give what should be given."

And that was his answer. Mary never did anything half-way. If she could not devote herself whole-heartedly, she would have to pass.

Reluctantly, Ben agreed to let things continue as they were. He could not imagine not having Mary in his life, at all, even though he ached to have her as his wife and soul mate. When they met, he knew she was special, that there weren't many like her around. What he didn't know, at that time, was just how special she was. He could not have imagined how he would grow to love her – to need her. At the end of his former marriage, suffering such hurt and anger, left alone with two very small children, he could not contemplate, ever loving or trusting again, but that was before he met Mary.

However the woman he most loved and desired remained elusive, always, just beyond his reach and maddening as it was, he could not give her up entirely.

FIVE

Mark and Eric were quiet and contemplative on the drive back from the Police Department. The meeting with Sgt. Mary O'Riley had depressed and discouraged them both. Not only did she not give the encouraging words they needed to hear, but she also seemed accusatory in her looks and tones. How could they be held responsible for this, each brother argued mentally? How could they, just by helping their younger brother, have contributed to his disappearance? How could their motives, which were unselfishly, if not purely driven out of love for their sibling, be called into question?

Finally, Eric broke the silence, "I don't think she liked us."

"What?" Mark asked, rather sharply, although he knew fully what his brother meant.

"Sgt. O'Riley. I don't think she liked us. For some reason, at least, I get that feeling."

"You may be right." Mark did not want to get in to this conversation for many reasons, not the least of which was he had been mentally questioning their handling of Tim's situation for a long time.

"Do you think it's our fault?" Eric pressed.

"No! Yes! I don't know! But, I'll tell you one thing, it makes me feel like Hell, and I'm not sure I want to talk about it – not now anyway."

With that, they were silent for the duration of the return trip to the West End. The few remaining minutes, seeming like hours. As his brother opened the door to exit the vehicle, he paused one leg in – one out. "It isn't our fault."

Mark chose not to respond to the remark, saying simply, "I'll call you."

He sat in his vehicle. Unable, it seemed to formulate or to process the necessary and required thoughts and actions needed to drive away. As he watched his older brother leave the parking lot in his new shiny Mercedes, he shook his head in disbelief. A wry smile crossed his lips, when it occurred to him why Eric had suggested he drive them downtown. That was his brother in a nutshell, never worried enough about anyone to stop worrying about possible damage to his new car. Finally, leaving the lot himself, he headed for his own home off River Road, a place he had lived with his wife for ten years now. He pulled into the broad driveway stopping his car outside their detached four-car garage, where he sat, reflecting on the events and the things leading up to them. When he entered the house, he was greeted by his wife of twenty-two years, Patty.

"Mark? You're back early."

"Hi," he said turning to face her in the foyer.

"My God, Mark. You look terrible. Come and sit down, I'll get you something to drink."

"Make it something strong, please."

"In the middle of the afternoon? Mark, are you all right?"

"I don't know Patty. I think I'm about to have some kind of a mental breakdown."

She came and sat down beside him, taking his icy hand in hers, rubbing it gently.

"Do you want to talk about this?" She knew without any words being said what was on his mind and she didn't think she wanted to say the words – so "this" was all that came out.

"I'm not sure. I mean, I guess I need to talk about 'this'. I need to voice my fears; my concerns; my anger. But, you may not be the best person. I really don't want you to witness my 'breakdown'."

"Mark. You and I have been through Hell and high water together. I think we can get through 'this'."

He started to say something, then changed his mind and just gave a sad shrug as he left the room. Patty knew not to press her husband. She would be waiting when he was ready to start talking to her about "this."

SIX

Mark had met Patty Smith during his first-year of internship at MCV Hospital, where she was working as a nurse. He had been so flustered the first day they met, he could tell she had sized him up as lacking what it took to become a doctor. With much dedication and application of considerable inner-strength, he had persevered and won her over. Though anything but an easy conquest, she now thought he was one of the most self-confident men she had ever met. For that reason, if no other, his words and appearance today were especially shocking. They had indeed been through a lot together. Finishing his internship, then a residency was no small feat. However, he did so while pursuing the woman who had caused feelings he had felt for no other, before or since. Patty was a strict adherent to "The Nurses Code", found at any teaching hospital, which included, " …and never, never, ever get involved with interns."

They were cocky, self-assured, self-assuming and they treated the nurses like second-class citizens. Usually, after some blue-eyed intern melted the resolve of this nurse or that one, they were gone – replaced by a new group of fresh med-school graduates, and the whole thing started all over again.

"Well, No thank you!" Had been Patty's response to Mark Addison's persistent, pestering and pleading.

"Why won't you go out with me?" Mark insisted one quiet afternoon, several months after they met. "Give me one good reason. Just one, I dare you."

"I can give you ten," Patty had snapped – not one to pass up a dare. "I don't date boys. I don't date interns. I don't date arrogant males, no matter what age. I don't date work mates. You don't have time to date. You wouldn't have the energy to date if you were doing your job. And, finally, I don't like you."

"Ouch! That hurts. And I don't think that was ten, probably more like seven or eight."

"Would you like me to go on?" she asked as she turned to face him with a rather wild-eyed look, which actually both scared and excited him.

"No. No, I think you have acquitted yourself adequately, Nurse Smith. I shall stay on my side of the desk in the future and I won't ask for any special favors. However, it may take me a while to work on the other aforementioned short comings and/or inadequacies. I'll get back to you in a decade or so."

"You do that."

SEVEN

Timothy Alan was the third and final child in the Addison family. With more than twenty years difference in age between himself and the oldest, Eric, there was never any secret in the household that his birth was unplanned – even unwanted, Tim felt most of his young life.

His parents had raised two boys – they were in their late forties when he was born; fifties, when he was ten; sixty, when he was a teen – and they seemed either too busy or just too tired to show much enthusiasm or interest in what he was doing.

Tim was a good child. Recognizing and accepting the need for quiet in the house from an early age, he was never noisy. His mother would be lying down with a cold compress on her head frequently when Tim came home from school, so the maid would let him in, fix his dinner and half-listen to his stories about the days activities.

Knowing fully that he never got the woman's full attention, Tim, who was a truly gifted boy, began telling her outrageous stories – lies, about what had happened at school. Such as, "…and then the aliens took us all on their spacecraft. But they brought us back by the end of school."

"That's nice," was her usual response. "Did you have fun?"

Finally, Tim tired of the game. Giving up trying, he ate his food in silence or while watching TV or reading. When Tim was thirteen, the maid quit and his parents didn't bother to replace her. Coming home after that to a dark and quiet house, he made himself a sandwich and went to his room, which had been moved downstairs – so as to give him some privacy, they said. Actually, he reasoned, it was so he would not disturb his mother, who seemed to be sick all the time now.

But, Tim, who was nothing if not resilient and adaptive, grew to like his little basement sanctuary. He had everything he needed to amuse himself – TV, Video Games, and a stereo, complete with headphones, of course.

From his teen years on, Tim Addison lived the life of a semi-recluse – leaving his room only for school, when he went to school and for food. He seldom saw his parents and he had no friends.

When Tim turned sixteen, he found himself in a couple of classes at school, which he actually enjoyed. Also, he was beginning to get a lot of positive attention from several of the really cute girls in his class – so he started dating and socializing a little. His parents didn't seem to care or notice when he came home, whom he was with, or what he was doing.

Tim tried pushing the rules – actually hoping to find out what they were or if there were any. At seventeen, he began drinking and staying out until the early morning hours.

His girlfriend at the time, Jeanette, a year older than he, was a little on the wild side herself, so she was only too happy to help Tim see what the limits were.

Everything got a little out of hand and Dr. Paul Addison was not amused to be summoned to police headquarters at five in the morning. After that, he paid a little more attention to what his youngest son was doing – for a while anyway.

Somehow managing to graduate from high school, Tim hadn't a clue what he wanted to do or become. He attended classes at Sargent Reynolds Community College, at Mark's insistence, for a couple of years, but nothing clicked. He got various jobs at local businesses – delivery work at one; stocking at a grocery store; even sales, which he was pretty good at.

By his twenty-fifth birthday, Tim had been in more than thirty job situations, which seldom lasted longer than a few months, except for the jobs in construction. He liked the physical labor and he especially enjoyed working out doors.

He developed a passion for skiing and hiking. He twice hiked the entire Appalachian Trail and he skied in Vermont, West Virginia, and Colorado. His father, thinking it was better for Tim to stay busy at something, funded his activities without question or debate.

Tim was good at everything he tried, landing a job as a ski instructor for several seasons in Colorado, which should have given him a start on his on. However, for some strange reason, he was drawn back to his basement retreat at the end of each season.

His brothers took him aside frequently, offering advice and money. They genuinely seemed to want him to get out of their parents basement and on his own. They funded technical school, job training, even counseling – which was a real trip to Tim.

"Is everything a joke to you Timmy?" Eric had demanded after getting a call from the therapist informing him that Tim wasn't cooperative or taking the sessions seriously.

"You're twenty-five years old," Mark had added. "Don't you think it's time you took a look at where you're going?"

"Hey. I didn't ask for your help. So why don't you both just go to Hell and take your checkbooks with you. I don't need the hassle. As for the therapy, it is a joke. That shrink is a pervert if you ask me. All he wants to talk about are my 'repressed sexual feelings.' Well I don't have any such repressed feelings – my sex life is fine. But, it's mine and I don't care to share details with any closet voyeur, thank you very much. Maybe all three of you should get a good roll in the hay. It would probably improve your outlooks on life."

Tim could never remember getting so upset with his brothers. But, then again, this was the first real confrontation, though far from the last, he had ever had with them. Now that their mother was apparently seriously ill, it seemed, the brothers were going to take up where his dad had left off.

Their mother died the following year. No one really seemed to know what she suffered from – but she had been sick almost all of Tim's life. He always assumed it was depression caused by his arrival at such a late date. Though, he still had many pleasant memories from when he was very young, before starting school, of a happy smiling mother who did things with him. He accompanied her on shopping trips to downtown Richmond at Thalhimer's and Miller and Rhoads and all the small stores on Broad Street and Grace Street. He especially liked to remember the scene at Christmas time. There would be a real nip in the air, a light snow falling, bell-ringing Santas at every store entrance. Tim was only too happy to drop coins in each of the buckets. His mother didn't seem to mind. However, it all changed and they no longer went shopping together. They no longer did anything together. His mother spent most of her time in her room with the heavy draperies closed, blocking out all the sunlight and with it any hope for happiness and a real future.

EIGHT

Tim desperately wanted – needed affection from his parents. He knew that much. By his early teens, however, he was pretty sure it wasn't coming. Strangely though, after his mother died, his dad began to rely on him. At first, he just seemed at loose ends, not sure what to do with himself now that his life's companion was gone. One day he wandered down to the basement, stood in front of Tim's door, seeming confused, almost lost.

"Dad?" Tim asked. "Are you alright?"

"Actually, Timothy, I think I'm rather lost. I mean, I can't seem to figure out how to get on with my life, without your mother."

"Come in, Dad. Sit down. I'll get you a drink."

Tim's response to his Dad's need was genuine and heartfelt, and the two actually became friends. They went out to eat together. Tim took his dad to the movies – something the senior Dr. Addison hadn't done in years. He also took him shopping at the mall.

"We gotta get you some new threads, Dad. You won't attract any babes in those thirty year old cardigans and cords."

"I didn't know I wanted to attract any 'babes' as you put it, Timmy."

"Come on Dad. You're still young. You've got a lot of life left in you."

His father was a trim, if not handsome man. He had a full head of hair, though it was gray now, and his health seemed good. They had fun shopping; though his dad resisted the idea of Wranglers and Tee Shirts, opting instead for Chinos and Polos. He also bought a hat, a jaunty little fedora, telling his son, "You know, I always used to wear hats. Everyone did. Now all you see are caps. No hats. I don't like caps."

"It's one of those dying traditions, Dad. But, who knows?" he added admiringly, "It looks pretty sharp, maybe you can get something started again."

The companionship did a world of good for both of them. Tim actually had a serious job now with a landscaping business. His dad went with him on some of his jobs, mostly the nearby-small ones.

"You know," his dad had offered one afternoon, "with a little investment in a truck and tools, you could do this for yourself, instead of working for someone else."

So Tim, with his dad as a silent partner, started Tim's Green Thumb Landscaping. With all the professional family connections, followed by a flurry of referrals because of his ability, not to mention his good looks, Tim was soon snowed under with calls from the local wealthy and mostly bored housewives, some of whom had more than just gardening in mind. In more than one case, Tim found himself in beds of linen and satin instead of shrubs and flowers. This flourish of activity lasted for almost four years.

Suddenly, with no warning, his dad had a stroke, and Tim seemed to collapse inward on himself. His business calls went unanswered, as he would not leave his father's side. Six months after the stroke, just short of five years after the death of his mother, Tim watched his father's coffin lowered into the ground and with it the only happiness of his life.

Eric and Mark tried to help. Mark and Patty invited Tim to their home for dinner; for watching games on TV; for tennis; swimming; anything and everything to try to get him out of his depression.

On one such visit, Tim announced to Mark, "I want to move out of the house."

"Why? Where?"

"I don't know, an apartment somewhere," he answered, ignoring the "Why?".

"What about the house. Now is not really a good time to try to sell it."

"I don't care. I can't stand being there anymore."

"Okay. Do you need money?"

"Wouldn't hurt." With that, the discussion ended, Mark took out his checkbook and wrote out a check for a generous amount of money to his brother, then went back to watching the game. They would discuss the house later. Their father's estate was tied up in probate, and there was very little liquid asset left, anyway – Tim and his dad had really spent a lot of money over the previous years. They were trying, it appeared, to make up for a lifetime of not being together in whatever time there was left.

Neither of the other brothers, at first, knew about the new relationship between their Dad and younger brother – they weren't involved. Eric, who was an unofficial watchdog of the family fortune, if it could be called that, got a tip from their accountant that a "lot of money" was being spent.

Their father's practice had been adequate, though far from lucrative, since he was located in the fan district, an area of Richmond where he saw numerous patients, many without insurance, who couldn't or didn't pay their bills. He would simply write it off. He never turned anyone over for collection, it wasn't his style. "If they can live with it," he said many times, "I can live without it."

However, when questioned by his son that perhaps he was spending too much, he snapped, "I guess I can spend it if I want. I earned it – and I see no point in leaving it for Marianne to spend shopping in New York." Those words ended the discussion of their father's spending.

NINE

No one in the family especially liked Eric's wife, Marianne. She was different. She was from New York, to which she needed to frequently, "escape" for shopping and recreation. She thought Richmond was far too Provincial, urging, nagging Eric to move them back to "The City." In her mind there was only one – and Richmond wasn't it.

Eric Addison, eldest son of the three, with two failed marriages behind him, had married Marianne, a beautiful divorcee with two young boys, when he was almost forty.

She was high-class. Just the sort of woman Eric thought he needed, unlike the other two who were both local girls with only average abilities and dreams, to help further his ambition and goals.

Eric wanted to get somewhere in his life; in his practice; and he saw Marianne as someone who could help him get where he wanted – the right person to be at his side for dinners and parties at the Country Club of Virginia, a place he would give his right arm, if not his first-born, to become a member. Surprisingly, with Marianne's New York connections putting a good word, in just the right ear, it appeared that being elected to membership was a real possibility. He could not have been happier.

Marianne was vocal, if not critical, from the beginning about the family dynamic (dysfunction, she really thought). "Why on earth does your mother stay in her room, in bed all the time?"

"Mother isn't well. She hasn't been for quite sometime."

"What's wrong with her? Your father and your brother are doctors for Christ's sake. Can't they figure out what's wrong and make her well?"

"No one seems to be able to determine what's wrong with Mother. It's almost as if she gave up on life."

"Why not take her to a specialist? There are plenty of those around. If not here in Backwater, USA, take her to Baltimore or DC. Someone, somewhere, should be able to do something."

"Mother doesn't travel well. I don't think she has been out of the house in over ten years."

"My God Eric! That's pathetic."

"Well. Dad has tried. He has had several physician friends of his come to the house to check her. She does have a weak heart – though not seriously so, I'm told."

"And what's the deal with your brother, Tim? He's the unseen, unheard person in the basement. Almost like the family's personal Hunchback. Doesn't he ever go out?"

"He does, I think, from time to time. He used to date quite a lot. Then he got into some kind of minor trouble. Dad had to go bail him out of jail in the middle of the night. And, well, that sort of ended his dating."

"How long ago was that? How old is he, anyway?"

"Let's see. I'm thirty-nine, so that means Timmy is nineteen. I guess it was two years ago when all that happened."

"God. I can't believe they live like that. And yet, you and your brother Mark seem, fairly normal."

"Mark and I grew up in a different family, almost. It wasn't like it is now, at all. Mother was very active. Dad still had his practice. I guess everything changed when Tim was born – or shortly thereafter. I think the shock of a baby at their age was just too much."

"Why didn't she have an abortion? Obviously the ordeal was a catastrophic event."

"Not an option. Mother and Dad are categorically opposed to abortion."

"Welcome to the Dark Ages. Here I thought y'all folks down south had gotten enlightened." She said in her best-faked southern drawl.

"Come on, Marianne. That's not even fair. Lots of educated people oppose abortion. It's a very complicated issue. For Mother and Dad, well, they are of another age, that's all."

"My point, exactly. The Dark Ages."

Marianne left the room which characteristic flair, letting her parting words close and seal the discussion. She was right. He was wrong. End of discussion.

TEN

Paul Addison met Dorothy Phillips when they were undergraduates at the College of William and Mary. He was in pre-med, she studied music. Both were from Richmond – though he had grown up in Lakeside, a mostly working-class neighborhood, while she was raised in the upper class area of the west end near the University of Richmond.

Dorothy was an only child. Her father was a successful corporate lawyer in an old prestigious Richmond law firm. Her mother was a successful interior designer, early on, then a socialite stay-at-home wife, in keeping with her husband's new position in the firm.

Her childhood was not unhappy, exactly, though she was frequently sad and had mild depression. She had all a young Richmond girl could want, all the things that should have made her happy – a pony when she was eight; tennis lessons starting at thirteen; a coming out party at sixteen; poolside Coke parties with her girlfriends at the country club.

After graduating from an exclusive private girls school, she decided Williamsburg would be her choice for continued study. Her mother had promoted the idea of a music conservatory in New York, where she could study voice. However, the idea of New York City did not appeal to Dorothy, at all. When she arrived at William and Mary, she knew she had made the right decision.

With her friends in Richmond, there was never any serious conversation. Just the same old, who was going out with whom? Who was now driving what? Who just got back from vacation where? Who was wearing the latest whatever?

She knew there should be more to life, even though she wasn't sure what it was, until now. For the first time, she felt happy.

Her roommate, Carolyn White, who quickly became her best and dearest friend, was from southern West Virginia, where she had graduated Valedictorian of her class and was attending college on scholarship. Her father owned a store; her uncles and cousins worked in coal mines.

Dorothy never tired of listening to the stories Carolyn would tell about the people and the hard way of life in Appalachia. It all seemed foreign to her. Yet, as she listened, she felt as if she were there – walking along a railroad track or going barefoot in a creek, turning over rocks looking for crawdads; she could almost feel the silky coal dust between her toes and smell the pungent fragrance of the blooming mountain laurel.

She had always felt slightly uncomfortable with the affluence and excesses of her family's way of life – almost embarrassed and apologetic. Now, she knew why. She had been shielded from the harsh realities of the inequities of life until she met Carolyn White.

Dorothy traveled home with her friend over spring break, seeing firsthand what poverty was all about. She saw people living, as if locked in a previous century, without indoor plumbing or central heat, in mere shacks perched on the sides of the mountains, or marching in formation along the creek bank, or clustered in a coal camp. Children in ragged clothes played in muddy creeks along the side of the dirt roads. For a moment, she thought she had been transported to some underdeveloped country. This certainly could not be the United States of America – with its car in every garage and chicken in every pot. Most of the residents of McDowell county of West Virginia didn't even have cars let alone garages to park them in.

Compared to their neighbors, however, the Whites were wealthy. They lived in a comfortable, albeit modest two story white house with facilities inside and a central heating system.

Carolyn's parents were just as friendly as their daughter of whom they were quite obviously and duly proud. At first they seemed a little uncomfortable having the child of true Richmond socialites as a houseguest. However, they soon found her friendly and easy to be with as Carolyn had assured them they would.

Dorothy enjoyed her vacation with the Whites more than any trip she could ever recall, including her graduation present of traveling abroad. Her parents were amazed if not mystified by their daughter's decision to go to the rural area of Appalachia – but that was their daughter always out to surprise them.

During her third year at William and Mary, Dorothy met Paul Addison, who was dating a friend of Carolyn's on a non-steady basis. She didn't especially like Paul at first. She found him to be rather cold. However, Paul was obviously quite smitten by Dorothy and began an all-out pursuit. When she finally agreed to go out with him for a Coke, he was so happy he could have sung.

At first, they were very awkward with each other. He wasn't sure what to talk about and she wasn't doing much better.

"I'm sorry," she offered. "I'm afraid I'm a little bit nervous this evening."

"I'm a lot nervous," Paul responded.

"What did you say you're major is?" she asked hoping to fill the awful silence.

"Pre-med. How about you?"

"Music education. I hope to teach music in the rural areas of the state."

"Do they even teach music in those areas? From what I've read, they're so under funded that music is a luxury they can't afford."

"Actually, most of the schools have some semblance of Music Education – though it's usually as marching band, which really would not be my preference."

"I can't exactly imagine you on the football field directing the uniformed-parade of would-be musicians."

"Me either. Choir is more my speed. There is some of that."

And with this exchange, they began actually talking easily. "You know," she said as if she had just had a brilliant idea. "A young doctor could also make a huge difference in that area."

He noticed the dancing eyes drop though, and the appearance of a flush, when he responded, "Why that almost sounds like some sort of a proposal."

He was sorry for the words, however, when she lowered her head.

"I'm awfully sorry for that remark," he offered.

"It's all right," she responded with little conviction in her voice.

Even with the derailing of their first date, she did agree to go out with him again. She found she liked being with Paul and it was obvious he liked being with her. They went to all the on-campus activities: Plays, poetry readings, debates, and discussions.

As their final year arrived, Dorothy's depression returned. She forced herself to keep up with her classes and activities. However, when graduation approached, she and Paul realized their relationship had not progressed to a level where they knew what to do next.

"I got a job," she informed him a few days prior to the commencement exercises.

"Where?" came his one-word reply, the sharpness of which surprised even him.

"In West Virginia."

"That's awfully far away."

"No it isn't, silly."

"With me at Medical School in Richmond? We'll probably never see each other again."

"Yes we will. My parents are in Richmond. I'll be coming there often. And we can write."

He got very quiet then looked at her in all seriousness, saying. "Dotty. I think I'm in love with you. I don't know if I can stand to lose you."

Nothing more was ever said of the job in West Virginia. Though Dorothy was sorely disappointed by not being able to realize her ambition of working with the underprivileged of Appalachia, she could not walk away from the feelings she also had for Paul. She wasn't sure if she was in love with him, exactly. She didn't know what to call the feelings. However, she knew she didn't want to lose him.

ELEVEN

Dorothy took a job in a Henrico County elementary school, which offered a fairly advanced music program. She enjoyed working with the children – even though they were from mostly middle to upper-middle class families, not the underprivileged she had hoped to work with.

Paul started working toward his medical degree in all seriousness, finding to his surprise that he had little time for any outside activities.

In spite of the joy she found in teaching, she was frequently depressed and even angry. "I may as well be in West Virginia," Dorothy said in one of those moments. "I almost never see you."

"I know. I'm sorry. Maybe when I get through this semester things will slow down a little."

"That's highly unlikely. Next semester will bring a whole new load of things. Then there is next year, then the next. And after you finish there's your internship, then your residency. Do you realize how many years that is?"

"Why don't we get married?"

"Are you out of your mind? You don't have time for a girlfriend, let alone a wife."

"Yes. But, it could make things easier. We would be together, anyway."

"No! It wouldn't. I would just be sitting at home waiting for my husband; resenting the amount of time you were spending in classes and in the labs. I would feel neglected; then become bitter; then we would divorce. No thank you."

"Then where do we go from here?" He asked in all seriousness.

"I don't know. But, it sure won't be to the altar."

They made it through his first year of study. After that, it was too much of an effort trying to be together, so Dorothy tearfully ended their relationship.

Paul Addison was stunned and angry, even though he knew she was right. This wasn't fair to either of them. He didn't have time for a serious relationship. But he wanted her – he just didn't know if he wanted the study of medicine more.

After spending a week mostly in bed, she decided to go to West Virginia to spend the summer with her friend Carolyn White and hopefully, she thought, to get out of her foggy mental state and to forget about Paul Addison.

Summer in the mountains did little to help her mood. The days were hot and unbearable. The evening and nighttime thunderstorms were unsettling – if a bit cooling.

Finally, a break came in the oppressive heat – she and Carolyn talked, read and took long walks along the railroad and in the mountains. It was almost like she remembered from her earlier visits.

Realizing she still cared, she wrote letters to Paul. At first he responded promptly, pleading passionately for her to come back to Richmond. Then his writing frequency decreased, then ended.

In the fall, deciding against returning to Richmond, she took a position, teaching literature (her college minor) and choir, in an area high school. Carolyn was teaching social studies at the same school so they spent much of their free time and work time in each other's company.

There were a couple of unmarried male teachers at the school who gave her admiring looks and began showing up at places she and Carolyn frequented. She went to the movies a couple of times with one science teacher – Bob Sweat. They had fun. They talked and laughed. Unfortunately, she realized, almost too late, that Mr. Sweat wanted something from her that she really didn't want to give.

Getting out of his car with what dignity she could muster, she walked away down the lake road on unsteady legs. She was angry at herself for not having seen where this was going. Her head was still spinning from the wine they had consumed. She knew she was going to be sick.

Bob Sweat was also angry – though for different reasons as she pushed him away, managing to back out of the car, at the last moment, driven by the high voltage like jolt to her system, when his apparently well trained hand found its way up under her skirt, touching her where no man's hand had been before.

He was not that much of a cad, however, so he regained his composure enough to realize that he could not allow her to walk the several miles home. Besides, he would have to face her at work.

"Dammit," he said to himself. If she wasn't that kind of girl, she could have said so. She didn't have to lead him on with her sexy way of turning her head. And that smile.

God, what a smile, he thought as he took another drink of the warm wine – which now tasted more like warm water, he thought. He started the car and drove down the narrow dirt road overtaking her quickly.

"Look. I'm terribly sorry," he said jumping out of the car and walking beside her.

"Well you ought to be," she said with a sniff.

He took her arm in his hand and turned to face her. Then he saw the tears.

"God. I feel like a real creep. You're probably the nicest girl I've ever gone out with. I had no right to treat you like that. Say you forgive me."

His plea seemed sincere enough, she thought. And the idea of walking in this heat with shoes that were killing her feet was not appealing.

"Please," he begged falling to his knee. "I will have to end my life right here, right now if you don't forgive me."

"OK."

She gave him a smile along with another sniff, and was forced to laugh when he dropped his head without rising saying, "Thank you my lady. I will be you humble servant henceforth, and forever."

While she doubted the sincerity of these remarks, she did like him. "Get up out of the dirt, will you? Now you're making me feel guilty."

TWELVE

She and Bob Sweat remained friends, though she declined all of his requests for further dates. She didn't think she could trust him or the feelings he stirred up within her. At the end of the term, he left the school for a better paying job in D.C.

Dorothy remained at her job in West Virginia for another three years. She dated little, spending most of her free time with Carolyn and her family. During the summer months, the two of them traveled around the country.

She made an important discovery the last summer they traveled. She realized her depression and unhappiness were an indication of something missing in her life. Something she had hoped to find by working where she felt she was needed. In the end, however, she decided, sadly, that one person could do little to improve the situation in Appalachia, and she personally could make little or no difference. Even more importantly, she realized that whatever it was that was missing in her life, it was up to her to find out, first of all, and that she alone had to fix it. No one else could do that for her.

Leaving the mountains behind, she returned to Richmond and the West End home of her parents, where she felt more alone than ever before in her entire life. Her father was almost never there.

"Your father's working late again," her mother would say, as she poured herself the first of several pre-dinner highballs, though she doubted it was really true. Even her mother seemed always to have a full day of activities planned.

Dorothy withdrew from life, after an ill-fated attempt at picking up where she left off with some of her old friends at the Club. They seemed even more inane now that they had married and were only interested in social climbing than they had in high school.

"Could you believe the dress she wore…" One conversation favorite seemed to be.

The insane giggles, waving of their cigarettes and giving her pitying looks over their martini glasses was just the final thing. "Poor Dottie," they offered with faux sympathy. "We just must find you a husband."

So Poor Dottie stopped going to the club and she didn't return phone calls – even those from her one true friend Carolyn White, whose wedding invitation sat unanswered on her desk.

She spent the next several months on the patio of her parents home, reading and rereading the classics as well as some more current writers: Thomas Wolfe; Hemingway; Fitzgerald; Faulkner. Then she discovered Ayn Rand, whose radical ideas of Capitalism and selfishness as a virtue seemed rather heartless, yet captivating. The bleak world and life situations presented by Carson McCullers did little to improve her moods.

Dorothy felt like she was drowning and there was no one there to help her out or throw her a lifeline. She began sleeping more and she contemplated suicide, feeling that only the finality of her death would bring her suffering to an end.

The well-meaning family doctor had given her a prescription for sleeping pills during one of her bouts with anxiety and insomnia. In the late hours of the night, just before dawn, Dorothy poured the pills out in her hand and swallowed them with a glass of water. Fortunately for her, the new maid was rather more like a drill sergeant than a servant.

Every morning at nine if Dorothy had not risen earlier, which had not been the case of late, she knocked on the door. Then she strode across the room with all the cheer she could muster, announcing as she threw open the drapes, calling, "Rise and shine, Missy. Time to get up and thank the Good Lord for a beautiful new day."

However, this morning, Dorothy did not respond when she walked over to the bed.

"Oh, no. Oh, God, no," the woman wailed as she picked up the telephone advising the operator of the emergency.

The curtains were drawn in the dimly lit room at Stuart Circle Hospital, so she could not make out the features of the person sitting beside her bed when she opened her eyes. She knew it wasn't her father. The figure was a much younger person.

She forced her eyes to focus on the now smiling face in response to the "Hi. How are you feeling?"

"Paul? Is that really you?" she asked in disbelief.

"None other," he answered.

"What are you doing here?"

"Well. I'm a resident here and I was on duty when they brought you in yesterday. I could not believe it was you on that stretcher. I felt like someone had just sucked all the air out of the room. I thought I was going to need a stretcher myself. After they admitted you, since my shift was almost over, I asked a buddy to cover for me. I came here, unable to leave you. So, that's why I'm here."

She seemed embarrassed to see him this way. This wasn't how she had hoped to see him again.

"Now that you're out of danger, suppose you tell me why you are here," he continued.

"I'm not sure I know the answer to that."

"Try," he said reaching out to take her hand.

THIRTEEN

After her release from the hospital, Dorothy's parents took her to what they referred to as, "...someplace nice." Where she could get some rest.

They arrived at an unimposing facility that looked something like a country home near Staunton in the Shenandoah Valley. Her parents had been extremely nervous and ill at ease around her since "the incident", as they referred to it. She felt they would be glad to dump her on someone else. But she didn't care.

The place was nice enough. The grounds were beautiful – she enjoyed walking through the gardens and talking to the old gardener whose name was Joe. In fact it was Joe who helped her regain some of her balance.

She started helping in the gardens. Digging and planting things was very therapeutic and it appeared, at least to Dot, as she now called herself, and Joe that she was good at it. She developed a real passion for working with plants and flowers.

She had received several letters from Paul. However, she didn't seem to have anything particular to say to him, so she didn't answer. He professed that he still loved her. That no one else would ever make him feel the way she did. At first, however, these were just words on a piece of paper – she could attach no particular significance to them, nor could she clearly remember the events to which Paul made reference.

After a few weeks of hard work in the gardens, though, things began to change. She found herself thinking of Paul and of her friend Carolyn White. She began to remember the feelings she had had for Paul and it seemed after re-reading his letters several times that she still had feelings for him. Therefore, she wrote Paul asking him to come visit her.

The Saturday of his visit, Dot was extremely nervous. She hadn't been this nervous in weeks. It was Joe's day off, so there was no work to do in the garden. She became agitated and paced the floor of her room most of the morning. Close to noon, she was informed that she had a gentleman visitor.

She looked at herself in the full length mirror, smoothed the nonexistent wrinkles in the skirt of her dress for the dozenth time; patted her hair and reapplied lipstick before descending the stairs in rather grand fashion.

Paul Addison was amazed at the vision of loveliness coming down the stairs to greet him. She was smiling in a way that could light up a whole room. He suddenly felt weak in the knees.

"Dottie," he finally managed. "You look lovely."
"Hello, Paul," she responded rather formally, he thought. "You are looking well also. Come. Let's go for a walk in the garden."

"All right."

"It was so good of you to come, Paul," she said after walking out of the building. "I have wanted to talk to you." Paul was a bit unnerved by the slow deliberate wording of her sentences. However, he decided that she must just be nervous. He knew he certainly was. They walked down the pebbled path which curved around a small lake to a white bench under some huge willow trees.

Paul looked into her eyes and was startled to see the fire he had marveled at was no longer there. She smiled at him, which seemed to prompt some of the warmth to resurface, but it wasn't the same.

"Dottie," he began, but she interrupted.

"Please call me Dot. I think I prefer that these days."

"OK," he responded, if a little uncertainly. "Dot."

After saying it, he decided he liked it – it seemed to fit the new look – the shorter hair; the makeup; the new style of dress – soft cotton with a full skirt.

"Dot," he resumed, "you said you wanted to talk to me. What is it you wanted to tell me?"

"Oh, I'm not sure, Paul. It's just that I've been re-evaluating a lot of things the past few weeks. I've read and re-read your letters dozens of times. I do care for you, Paul. I can't abide the feeling of making you feel unhappy. I've experienced so much true unhappiness, I wouldn't wish that for anyone. I'm just not sure how to pick up the pieces and go on. In many ways, I want to get on with my life. However, I like it here. I feel safe and comfortable and I'm afraid those feelings will go away once I leave. Yet, I know I can't stay here forever. That's unrealistic."

Paul noticed her hand was trembling as she smoothed her hair. He took her hand in his, kissing it gently. How could he have allowed this to happen to the love of his life?

How could he have let the study of medicine or anything else take priority over this delicate flower.

"Dottie, I'm so sorry for what you've been through. I feel it's my fault. I should have been there for you and I wasn't. I want you to be my wife. Say you will marry me and come away from here with me. Please."

"Paul. I care for you deeply. I'm just not sure I'm ready to say yes to marriage. Will you please give me a little time? I need to work things out in my mind."

FOURTEEN

Paul and Dorothy were married in the fall of that year. He finished his residency and went into private practice, first with two other doctors, then on his on. He structured his work and patient load so that he could spend adequate time with his new wife, who seemed genuinely happy.

She had a small garden, then a small greenhouse, then a larger greenhouse. Growing things was truly therapeutic – her main remedy for keeping the sadness at bay.

She announced to her husband one quiet afternoon that they were going to have a baby. Paul was elated. She was concerned. However, the pregnancy went smoothly, the baby boy – Eric was healthy. Fortunately, she was too busy with the new baby to be sad.

Another son, Mark was born just short of two years later. He also was a healthy baby.

As both boys grew and flourished, Dorothy allowed herself to relax. It seemed she had been holding her breath, afraid of what was to come.

Eric and Mark were active, normal boys. They played touch football with their dad. They joined the Scouts. They grew. They were happy. When the boys were in their teens, a familiar fog began to creep in to Dorothy's life. At first it was just a wisp, which was barely noticeable. Then it became a shroud which enveloped her threatening to suffocate her.

Paul came home one afternoon when Eric was preparing to start college. The house was dark and quiet, even though her car was in the drive, she was not around.

"Dot," he called from the foyer. "Honey? Are you here?" Panic began to seep in to his being. He charged up the stairs, throwing open the bedroom door.

"Dot?" he called into the dark room, groping for the light. He fell to his knees at the sight of his wife in bed. "Dot. Honey. Wake up. It's me."

He telephoned the hospital calling for an ambulance. He rode beside her holding her hand and stroking her hair. She was his world and he felt it slipping away.

FIFTEEN

The doctor who examined her could not explain why she could not be roused. There was a trace of sleeping medication in her system, though not enough to cause concern. She seemed to have a slight heart irregularity, but that too was minor.

The two men walked out into the hallway. "By the way," he asked Paul, "Did you know your wife is pregnant?"

"Pregnant? No. That's not possible. I mean I guess it is possible, but we thought she was menopausal. Are you certain?"

"Quite certain. She is probably about ten to twelve weeks."

Paul's head was reeling. Pregnant? A child at their age? He was almost fifty. Dot was only a year younger. How could this be? How could he let this happen? He was certain he remembered the occurrence. They both had been feeling rather "frisky" was how she had described it. Both the boys were gone for the weekend. They had spent a rainy Sunday afternoon in bed.

Dorothy was never quite the same. However, she became irate when her doctor suggested she consider an abortion. That was unthinkable. She became very thoughtful and quiet during the next few months. Paul was not sure what to say or do.

After the birth of the child, Paul hoped her situation would improve at the sight of their third healthy son – Timothy.

Paul hired a housekeeper to help with the running of the house and caring for the baby. Dorothy watched quietly as her son grew. For several years, she spent time with Timmy: reading books to him; playing games; and taking him downtown for shopping – something they both enjoyed. She realized he was different from his brothers. He played different games, liked different toys. Tim was a quiet sensitive boy and as he approached school age, she lamented to Paul as the depression crept in, that she could not believe what she had done.

"What is the problem?" Paul asked her completely confused.
"Don't you see?" she cried. "He isn't going to be like Eric and Mark. Not like you. He is going to be like me. Sad. Lonely. Depressed. How could I have let this happen? I just want to die."

"Dottie. Please. He will be fine."

How he wished he could convince her and himself that he believed this. Tim was different. It was obvious. He tried playing catch with Timmy – but he was a little to old and stiff to chase the balls. He encouraged the boy to join the Scouts, but Timmy wasn't really interested.

"No thanks," had been his answer.

Tim turned to his books and his thoughts and began his own solitary, lonely existence, while his parents looked on, unable to offer any alternative. He was in charge of his own routine mostly. He got up. Went to school. Came home. Sometimes, when his mother was feeling well, be would go into her bedroom and talk with her. He enjoyed those times, but they were rare.

Dorothy's depression along with her other, seemingly minor ailments, were now her constant companions. Paul tried everything he could think of to stop the demise of his life's love. But, nothing seemed to work. He took her back to Staunton for help, with little or no success. Her world – her life had ended. Her husband and her son stood by – helpless.

SIXTEEN

Paul Addison gave up his practice, turning it over to his son Mark, who had joined him a few years earlier. It really wasn't much of a decision – he had been mostly absent from the office for the past year, never wanting to leave Dorothy's side.

Mark did not complain or question. He just picked up the slack – becoming familiar with his father's patients and learning to work a little bit faster, he could make it work. Some of the patients, the older ones especially, missed Dr. Paul. However, Dr. Mark, with his winning smile and friendly manor soon won them over.

Shortly thereafter the University expansion consumed even more buildings in the historic Fan District – the offices of the Doctors Addison among them. Mark relocated the practice to the far west end of the city on Patterson Avenue. Dr. Paul Addison, though his name remained on the door, and his son provided a spacious office for his father, made no semblance of effort at being a part of the practice. His days were spent sitting mostly and watching the life of his wife slowly slip away.

One day in despair, he cried to no one in particular, "What the Hell good is medicine anyway? If you can't cure the one closest to you, what the Hell is it all about?"

Dr. Paul Addison found himself succumbing to his wife's depression. He no longer wanted to live. He no longer shaved everyday, as had been his custom for almost fifty years. He no longer read the *Times-Dispatch*. The papers collected in the foyer till the maid would throw them out, as they had arrived - rolled-up and unread. Saddest of all, Paul Addison sometimes did not speak to or even see his son, Tim, who was now in his mid-teens, for days.

The boy seemed self-sufficient. He came and went – never seeming to have any particular needs. His father gave him a generous allowance at the beginning of each week. Tim rarely asked for more till the beginning of the next week. Paul realized, however, that all was not well with his son and that attention was needed when a four a.m. telephone call from police headquarters informed him that Tim and a female companion had been arrested. The charges of drunk and disorderly were like a slap in the face to his father.

When he arrived at the Department, Paul had not decided what he wanted to say to his son, simply asking, "Are you all right?"

"Yeah," was his only response.

They drove home without talking. Tim suspected his dad was probably raging inside. However, when they got home, he was surprised that no lecture seemed forthcoming.

"Dad?" he attempted to break the horrible silence.

His words were stopped with his father holding up his hand and simply saying, "We'll talk later," as he started up the stairs.

Though the talk never occurred, the disappointment and confusion in his father's eyes were more than enough to curb Tim's excesses. He returned to his solitary life and confinement in the basement of his parents' home.

Tim graduated from High School the following summer. His father, brother Mark, and Patty represented his family in attendance. Eric and Marianne were in New York and his mother was too ill to attend.

Mark and Patty, after their father excused himself to get back to Dorothy, took Tim for a celebratory dinner. Efforts at conversation by Mark and Patty were generally met with monosyllabic responses.

Mark, near the end of the dinner, made one last effort. "Timmy," he started with such suddenness that both Tim and Patty were startled. "Patty and I have been uncertain what to give you for your graduation gift."

He paused almost as suddenly as he had started, causing Tim to feel that some response was required. "No problem," Tim offered.

Mark pulled an envelope from his pocket and continued. "However, we have decided that you probably should go somewhere. Anywhere you choose," he finished handing the envelope to his brother.

Tim opened the envelope and found a travel voucher from a local agency entitling the bearer (Timothy Addison) and companion of choice two round-trip tickets, by the conveyance of choice to a destination of choice. Accommodations included.

Tim was speechless. He had just been given a blank check to go anywhere in the world that he wanted. He looked at his brother then at Patty, a tear formed in his eye as he tried to speak. "I don't know what to say."

"You don't have to say anything," Patty answered reaching across the table taking his hand in hers.

"Thanks. Thanks a lot. I've thought about traveling. Really. I've thought about it a lot. I just wasn't sure where or how to start. I still don't. But now I'll figure it out. Thanks. Both of you have always been good to me – but this is, well, it's just awesome."

"You're welcome," his brother added.

After the dinner, they invited him home with them. He declined, saying with more emotion and excitement than they had seen before, "I got things to do. Plans to make."

"Who are you going to take with you?" Patty asked innocently enough.

Doubt and uncertainty replaced the happiness in his eyes, making her wish she could kick herself and take back the question. When his smile returned, she allowed herself to relax.

"I haven't even thought about that – probably no one."

Patty gave Tim a hug and kiss which seemed to make him uncomfortable again – but then he relaxed and smiled. His brother opted for a handshake for which Tim was grateful.

"Call us," she demanded as they parted company.

"I will," he promised.

SEVENTEEN

The light in the den, an unusual occurrence, caught his attention as he drove up to the modest home of his parents. He went upstairs without even stopping in his room. He found his father sitting, looking at nothing, in the quiet room.

"Dad? Are you OK?"

"Huh? Oh, hi Timmy. I didn't hear you come in. Did you have a nice time?"

"Yeah. It was good. Mark and Patty are," he searched for the right word – something he had not tried to do before, "They're, OK," he concluded.

"Yes. They are," his father agreed.

"Mother all right?"

"Yes. She's resting."

"You will not believe what Mark and Patty are giving me as a graduation gift."

His father seemed confused by this statement. Or was it a question, he wondered, as he looked at his son. It had not really occurred to his father that a gift was required. How really strange, he thought to himself.

"They have given me a travel voucher."

"A what?" the elder man asked seeming genuinely confused.

"A travel voucher. I can go anywhere I want – anytime. Isn't that the greatest?"

"Yes. It certainly is. Where are you going?" he asked, responding sincerely to his youngest son's rare display of enthusiasm.

"I don't know yet. I've got to decide, though. I want to go soon, I think." Then as he rose to leave the room, a thought occurred.

"Dad?"

"Yes?"

"They said I can take someone with me."

"That's nice. A traveling companion is always good. Who are you going to take?"

"I'm not sure. But, I was wondering," he paused looking down at the floor. "Dad. Would you like to come with me? I mean, I know it's sudden. And with Mom's situation, it's not easy for you to get away. But, it could be good for you."

"Oh, I couldn't possibly leave your mother. But, thanks for asking."

"Sure, Dad," he said trying to conceal the disappointment he was feeling.

"Goodnight," he said, leaving the room.

"Huh?" His father seemed to have already returned to his private thoughts – no doubt reliving the years of his youth with his wonderful and beautiful Dottie. When he looked around, the room was empty; he was alone.

EIGHTEEN

Summer turned into fall and Tim still had not decided where he wanted to go. His mind had started spinning the moment he had seen the voucher, which he had re-read several dozen times since. He wanted to take his dad on the Canadian Railway tour he had read about. It hadn't even occurred to him that his father would not even consider going.

At first he was hurt, then disappointed, then angry – at both of them; angry at her for taking to her bed so many years ago, for no obvious reason; angry at him for his stubborn refusal to leave her side, his refusal to admit that she had already left him and his refusal to get on with his life.

The fact that his father never even mentioned the discussion also made Tim angry.

Was his offer of so little consequence that his father could dismiss it offhandedly without so much as a serious response?

On one of his frequent visits that summer to Mark and Patty's, he started to mention the situation to his brother, but then dismissed it, when asked, "So. Have you decided where? When? And with whom?"

"No," he answered, without further comment.

"Well, there's no hurry," Mark offered. "There's no expiration date on the offer," he added giving his brother a reassuring pat on the back as he passed his pool-side patio chair on his way into the room adjacent. "You want a beer?"

"Sure."

"Are you going to enroll in college?" Mark asked offering him a cold bottle of beer.

"I'm not sure?"

"You could take a couple of classes at Reynolds and see how it goes."

"I don't know if I want to go back to school. I'm thinking about going to Colorado."

"Colorado?"

"Yeah. I might like to learn to ski. I mean you said, anytime, anywhere."

"I know. But, I really was thinking of someplace a little more exotic than Colorado."

"Hey. Colorado's exotic. You ever been to Aspen?"

"No. I've never been to Aspen. Though, I'm sure Marianne goes there frequently."

"Does Marianne ski?"

"I doubt it," he said with a wicked chuckle. "The clothes would make her look fat and the hat would mess up her hair."

"And she might break a nail," Tim responded in kind. They both broke into riotous laughter as Patty came out to the patio.

"Is this a private joke? Or one you can repeat in mixed company?"

"Oh," Mark said, trying to stifle his laughter and amusement at his sister-in-law's expense. "I guess it's rather private," he continued unable to contain his laughter.

"Very private," Tim added, with little more success than his brother at regaining composure.

"Men!" Patty snorted, shaking her head as she returned to the house, the howling laughter of her husband and Tim following behind her. Secretly, she was pleased to see such good humor – a rare event between the two brothers and wished for more of the same. Also, having heard their comments about Marianne, she was likewise finding it hard to keep a straight face. Marianne was just far too amusing in her disdain of all things about the South in general and Richmond in particular. You had to laugh at her – otherwise, you would have to take her seriously; then who could be around her?

"Colorado?" she heard her husband asking after the laughter had subsided.

"Yeah. Colorado," Tim added with awe, if not almost reverence in his voice. "Just think about it. The Rockies. The skiing. The excitement."

"The babes?"

"Now, who said anything about women in this picture?"

"Are you saying your fantasy doesn't include them?"

"Well, no. I'm not saying that at all. Maybe just a few."

"Just a few, huh?"

"One or two, maybe."

The brothers smiled at each other – each content in his own way with that moment. Happier and more at ease with each other than either could remember. They sat silent for several minutes it seemed just looking at the clear water of the pool. When Tim got up from his chair, Mark assumed he was on his way to the John. However, he suddenly became aware that his chair on the edge of the pool had received a body-slam from his younger brother. Before he could respond or brace himself, he and his chair hit the water with a mighty splash.

"Oh, are you gonna get it," he spluttered as he surfaced.

However, much to his surprise and confusion there was no one on the patio. He looked around for his brother, a little confused, when suddenly he was hit from behind under water, knocking his feet and lower body out from under and sending him in a backward somersault.

Mark was not a natural swimmer. He could hold his own in a pool, but each time he regained his balance and upright position, he was hit again by his brother's torpedo-like action and accuracy.

Thinking to himself, '…this is war,' he realized that only by diving to the bottom of the pool could he hope to locate and retaliate against his attacker. The last attack had come from the front, so he reasoned Tim would be approaching from the rear at any second. Forcing his body into a spin, he dove to the side and headed for deeper water, just as his brother made contact and gave only a glancing blow. Mark had never liked having his eyes open under water without swim goggles, but he forced himself, so he could regain his orientation and form a counter attack. His strategy had worked. He saw his brother flip overhead and start his return attack where he thought his prey was still floundering in shallow water.

With all the force he could muster, Mark sprang from his squatting position on the bottom of the pool and with the arrow-like precision hit his now confused attacker in the thighs sending his lower body high above the water. Mark was impressed by the apparent success of his counter measures when his brother splashed as the flip was completed.

Tim, who was a good swimmer, though, and younger and more agile than his brother, regained his balance quickly and made his own run for deeper water. What ensued was a crude form of water ballet mixed with brotherly horseplay. The splashing had again brought Patty out of the house. She watched in amazement as the two alternately dove then sprang, grabbing a foot or leg or what other body part could be grasped, sending the other down into the water. At one point, she wondered momentarily if they were angrily trying to drown each other. The fact that neither was trying to escape but was responding in kind, relieved her fears.

Finally, Mark surfaced and held up his hand saying, "Uncle. You're too much for me."

"Oh, you're just old," his brother responded.

The two swam to the shallow end then stood up and started walking, wearily up the steps at the end of the pool. Mark put his arm around his brother's back as they cleared the last step. After a slight pause, Tim did the same. They walked down the patio toward Patty who stood smiling broadly at the two of them.

"You two look like wet dogs," she chided.

Mark looked down at his soggy shorts which hung around his legs and pulled his tee shirt, which clung to his chest. He realized he was exhausted as he watched his chest rise and fall rapidly.

Gasping for breath, he managed, "I guess I am old."

They collapsed on lounge chairs letting the sun dry their wet clothing. It was one of the most memorable afternoons either of them had ever experienced. As he was heading out the door much later, Tim stopped giving his brother a big hug.

"Thanks," he said.

"You're welcome," Mark responded. "Though next time you feel the need to drown someone, let me know in advance. I'll invite Eric."

Both laughed as Tim got in his car and started the engine.

"You got it."

NINETEEN

Richmond Ski and Scuba was a well known local supplier of all things relative to the two activities mentioned in the firm's name.

"Do you give skiing lessons?" Tim Addison inquired of the pretty young woman who greeted him.

"We most certainly do," she responded with a huge smile as she grabbed Tim by the arm. "Allow me to show you our classroom."

She guided him to the rear of the store and through a large portal into a room as big as a gymnasium. Fully-clad skiers practiced on the artificial slopes – treadmill-like inclines of varying angles, around the room.

"Wow!" Tim uttered in surprise as he looked around at the scenario of the refrigerated room.

"Isn't it something?" the young lady – who called herself, "...Geena, with double e's," asked while still holding on to his arm. "I get excited every time I come back here."

Loud music partially masked the barking of several of the instructors at their charges as they took tumble after tumble on the slopes.

"When can I start?"

"How about right now? One of the beginner slopes is open and I'm free for a lesson."

"Great. Let's do it."

"Come with me then. I'll show you what you'll need."

After two lessons at Richmond Ski and Scuba, Tim and "Geena, with 'double e's," went out for a meal and a movie. After six lessons, he was ready to move up to more advanced instruction, so Geena turned him over to Rob, "...just one O and one B," who suggested he do some weight training to build up his upper arm strength. And of course, Richmond Ski just happened to have a complete weight room.

The remainder of his summer and early fall were devoted to the pursuits of learning to ski, weight training, and of course – Geena, with two "e's," and a lot more attributes he had discovered, who was now a steady item in his life.

By mid-October, he decided it was time head west. Tim said goodbye to Geena, who seemed more than ready to move on to her next project, as he left Richmond Ski and Scuba for the last time.

Saying goodbye to his Dad and Brother Mark, was not as easy as he had expected.

"Hey. I'm not going to be gone forever," he responded to their looks. "I'll be back before you know it," he promised.

"I'll call you when I get there," he offered to Mark and Patty at the airport. Surprised by the degree of emotions he was feeling, he wiped away a tear as the United Jet roared down the runway and lifted off into the blue Virginia sky, banking north for its short hop to Dulles Airport, before heading on to Denver. It had really been a nice summer and early fall with Mark and Patty.

He hated to see it end. However, he was eighteen years old and wanted to see what life had in store.

TWENTY

Colorado was all that Tim had imagined and more. He drank in the vistas, filling his senses with the awe inspiring majesty of the mountains and the sky. He had never felt so alive in his entire life. On numerous days, he would just sit, or stand, and stare, trying to take it all in.

Reminding himself that he came here to ski, not just sightsee, he set about finding an affordable place to stay and hopefully like-minded individuals. A tip from a bellman at his hotel helped him locate a rooming house not far away, where several other adventure seekers were spending the winter.

He found a roommate and immediate friend in Karl Winters, who had just arrived from Georgia. They were about the same age. However, Karl, who was in fact only on his second trip to the Western Mountains, became Tim's self-appointed guide and expert on all things Colorado.

Tim discovered rather quickly that the artificial environment at Richmond Ski and Scuba had not completely prepared him for the real-life slippery slopes and obstacles of the ski runs. However, in typical persistent fashion after a day or two of falling down, when not colliding with other people and objects, he looked and felt like he had been skiing all his life.

"You're a natural at this," Karl praised as he limped into the rooming house.

"Yeah? Try telling that to my sore and bruised body."

"I keep telling you. You're supposed to land on your ass. That's what all the padding is there for."

"I know. But somehow, my arms and legs and head seem to be the parts of me that are most often making contact with the ground."

"Just remember. When you feel yourself losing it, just let go and sit down. Don't fight it. It only makes it worse."

Bruises and collisions were becoming part of his life – but they did little to dampen his enthusiasm and determination. After a month of practice, he felt it was time to advance from the beginner runs to something a little more difficult. He also concluded that part of his continued problems were the obstacles presented by the people on the slopes who were even more inexperienced than he.

When he informed Karl of his decision, his response of, "Well it's about time," was all the encouragement Tim needed.

Early the next day, they headed for the slopes and some serious skiing. One week and one broken leg later, after having concluded just perhaps he wasn't quite ready for such serious skiing, Tim was on a jet heading back to Richmond.

It was early January, so Tim decided to humor his brother and enroll in a couple of classes at Sargent Reynolds Community College. The classes were interesting enough, however, something still felt not quite right. Tim plodded through the semester finishing with unimpressive grades in each of the courses he had tried. Feeling that college wasn't the answer, Tim wanted to move on.

"But, you hardly gave it a fair trial," Mark countered. "Two courses isn't exactly a challenging endeavor. Nor is it representative of what college has to offer."

"Look, Mark. I'm sorry. I know you're only thinking about what you feel is best for me. But, I don't see college in my future."

"So what is in your future? Colliding with more boulders and trees?"

"Maybe. I don't know."

"Next time you know it could be that hard head of yours and not a limb."

"Hey. There's not a boulder or tree on this planet that could make a dent in this head."

"You're probably right there," his brother conceded with a shake of his own head.

"Cheer up Mark," Tim said putting his arm across his brother's shoulder, "I'm sure there is something out there waiting for me. I just have to find what it is."

"Are you sure you'll recognize it? After all, destiny is usually a bit more elusive than trees and boulders."

Patty had stepped into the room just as Mark finished his pronouncement, "Wow! My husband the philosopher. Is that an original thought?" she asked with all the sarcasm she could muster. "Aren't you being just a bit too pontifical? He's only been out of high school a year. Not everyone is fortunate enough to know where his destiny lies at the age of nineteen."

"Thanks Patty," Tim said with a hug. "I was beginning to feel the flames of Hell on my feet. You know the sin of indecision is the most deadly of all in the Addison Bible."

"Make fun, you two. You'll both feel differently when Tim is approaching thirty and still doesn't know what he wants to do," Mark predicted.

"My God, Mark. That's ten years from now. Surely you don't think it will take ten years for me to find my way."

"You wouldn't be the first person."

"Come on Mark. Lighten up. Will you? This is supposed to be a fun evening. Besides, the food's ready."

Mark's words had obviously hit a nerve with Tim. He was quiet and distant during dinner, in spite of Patty's attempts to bring him out of his state. When the meal was finished, he excused himself, saying he wasn't feeling too well and wanted to get home. Mark's attempt at apology did little to lighten the dark cloud that had descended over him.

TWENTY-ONE

Tim passed the season, after his broken leg healed, going from one menial job to another. He worked hard at whatever it was he was doing and he saved almost everything he made.

When winter approached, his latest construction job nearing an end, he wasn't sure what to do next. During one evening of particular indecision, his telephone rang.

"Hello?"

"Hey buddy, where the Hell are you? There's a tree up here with your name on it."

"Karl?"

"None other. How's the leg?"

"It's fine. How are you? Where are you?"

"Colorado. Wondering why I haven't heard from you."

"Sorry. I meant to call, but things have been kind of strange here."

"Hey. What you need is some of this thin mountain air to clear your head. Damn air in Richmond and Atlanta is too heavy to breath. Clogs up your mind."

"You're probably right about that. My thinking pipes feel like they need a good Roto-Rooter job."

"I'm telling you. All you need is some of this air, snow and the babes. Oh, man, you will not believe this one lovely creature I met yesterday. I'm telling you, it makes my heart flutter just to think about her."

"You sure it's your heart that's fluttering?" he responded with a laugh.

"Oh, absolutely! But, I mean this woman could well be the future mother of my children. It's definitely a heart thing. So, when you coming?"

"I don't know. I've been saving money all summer, though I wasn't sure what for."

"Well. What are you waiting for?"

"I have a couple of weeks left with the job I'm on right now. I guess I could leave after that."

"Now you're talking."

"OK, man. I think I will."

"Cool. I'll keep your space open."

"Karl, thanks for calling man. I mean this has been a rough few months. I guess I need a breath of fresh air. I'll call you when I'm heading out."

"Great. See you."

Tim hung up the phone immediately wondering how he was going to tell Mark about this. Angry with himself, he threw a book across the room muttering to the room, "Why the Hell do I have to explain or justify myself to Mark."

TWENTY-TWO

"You're sure you don't want me to wait with you," Patty asked him at the airport.

"Positive. You get back home. Thanks a million for dropping me."

"You're welcome," she said with a kiss as he leaned over.

"Do you have enough money?"

"Sure. I've got plenty. I haven't exactly had anything to spend money on the past few months."

"Well call me if you need anything. OK?"

"You bet. And Patty, thanks. You're one in a million."

"Oh, you're just saying that because you're mad at your brother."

"No. I'm really not. I mean it."

"Well, thanks," she said, feigning embarrassment. "Don't worry too much about Mark. He'll come around. You'll see."

"I don't know," he said as he continued unloading his baggage from the van. "He was pretty mad."

"Which airline?" the porter asked.

"United."

"If you have your ticket I can check you in here."

Tim handed the elderly black man his ticket folder with a smile. "Thanks."

He turned back to Patty who had gotten out of the van and stood beside him in front of the terminal.

"I meant what I said," she continued. "If you need anything, just call me."

He hugged his sister-in-law with all the emotion that he dared express in a public place. She wiped away a tear. He cleared his throat.

"Hey. It'll all be fine," he tried to be reassuring.

"I'm sure it will," Patty said as she instinctively brushed an unruly strand of hair back from his forehead. "Take care of yourself. You're a good kid."

"I wish everyone in this family shared your feeling."

"Sir," the porter interrupted. "Your plane will begin boarding at gate twelve in about thirty minutes."

"Thanks," he said with a smile taking his ticket and exchanging it for a five-dollar bill.

"Thank you young man," the old gentleman said with a smile. "You have a good flight. Ma'am," he said tipping his hat to Patty. "You have a good day."

"Thank you." She said with a sincere smile. "I'm going to miss you," she said to Tim.

"Me too. I've enjoyed all the meals and evenings with you and Mark and the girls. Give them both a hug and kiss from me."

"They're going to miss you. They both have a major crush on you."

"Wow. All the women who love me are either married or too young. I sure hope that isn't my destiny."

"I'm sure you'll find plenty of eligible women in Colorado."

"Let's hope so. Gotta go," he said giving her another quick peck to the cheek.

"Bye, Tim."

Patty stood at the curb watching as he waved and entered the terminal and as far as she could see him down the corridor. Then with a sigh, she walked around her vehicle feeling suddenly very sad and depressed.

Tim felt rather the same as he headed for gate twelve and United flight 212, departing at ten forty-five for Washington's Dulles airport and continuing on non-stop to Denver. The flight was boarding as he approached the gate waiting area. He took his place at the end of the line hoping his mood would lift soon.

"Good Morning," the gate attendant said without really looking at him as he took his ticket. "Have a nice flight."

He fought his way through the throng of passengers blocking the aisle attempting to stow what could have been all their earthly belongings in the overhead bins. He never understood the paranoia involved in refusing to check luggage. 'It's just clothing for gosh sake. It isn't the crown jewels...' he thought when he finally found his seat after stashing his single item of carryon luggage overhead. He thought it rather odd that the plane was totally full for a mid-week flight up to D.C. and on to Denver. Why are so many people leaving Richmond, he wondered?

"Ladies and Gentlemen," the voice of the flight attendant broke into his thoughts with the usual, "...welcome aboard flight 212, Boeing 737 Jet service for Dulles airport with continuing service on to Denver..."

Tim had flown enough that the pre-flight announcement rarely kept his attention. And from looking around the plane, he saw few other passengers paying attention. He wondered what would happen if they really needed some of that valuable emergency information being relayed. Would they have time to extract the cards from their seat-back pockets? Would they have time to locate the nearest window exit? Would they know how to use the oxygen masks if they descended? Could they strap on their seat cushion, which could be used 'incase of water landing as a floatation device?' He shook his head in amazement – so many people, so certain that they would reach their destination without needing any of the aforementioned important information. He thought, that's probably what it takes to board one of these flying cattle cars in the first place. He wondered how many of these bovine-like passengers would bolt and head for the nearest exit if the speaker suddenly screamed, "...now pay attention. I happen to know for a fact you are going to need this information during this flight..."

Life is kind of funny, he thought, the jet engine on his side of the plane coming to life, as the plane was pushed back from the terminal. People go through their day-to-day lives without thinking about "what-if". Always assuming that tomorrow will come along, just like today did, he reasoned, is just one more defense mechanism everyone uses in order to get by. Think of the chaos that would ensue if everyone who was going to die today knew it before hand. He imagined there would be a lot of heart-felt prayers, last minute attempts to bargain with God for, "… just one more day. Please."

Tim had not been raised with any particular religious training. His mother's family had been Catholic, his dad was Protestant, though he could not remember either of them ever attending church. Personally, he had concluded from his thoughts, reading and just general contemplation that God must exist; that all the beauty in the world had to indicate intelligent design. Whether God took an interest in the daily lives of humans, he wasn't sure about that one.

He had gone to the Methodist church a couple of times with Mark, Patty and the girls during the summer. He found the experience rather moving, over all. He felt a peaceful, even serene, kind of sensation come over him. He commented to Patty later, "…it was pretty awesome, actually."

"I'm glad," she had said with her usual smiling manner. Nothing more – no, " I hope you will go with us again…" No, "…do you want to talk to the priest," (or reverend or whatever he was). Just, "I'm glad."

That was Patty, he thought to himself with a smile. He knew why his brother had fallen for her the first time he laid eyes on that face; that smile; those eyes. Patty could make you feel warm all over with that smile. Yes, he thought. Mark was one lucky guy.

"Ladies and gentlemen…" the speaker interrupted his thoughts with a start which actually made his heart jump.

'What's this,' he thought; 'an actual emergency? Damn, I knew I should have read that card…'

"Ladies and gentlemen," the voice continued after what seemed an unusually long pause. "Please see that your seat belts are securely fastened in preparation for landing at Dulles International Airport. We'll be on the ground in just a few minutes."

He breathed a sigh of relief and promised he would find and read everything on the emergency information card.

TWENTY-THREE

Colorado rewarded Tim's senses every bit as much as it had on his first visit, if not more, when he stepped from the plane in Aspen. He stood for several minutes trying to absorb everything – the crisp dry air, the brilliant blue sky.

"Hey!" a familiar voice with a heavy Georgia drawl from among the throng caught his ear. "Son of a gun. If it isn't the old tree-cruncher from Richmond."

"Hey Karl," he said grasping his friend's outstretched hand.

"Well. I must say you're a sight. Man you like a tourist, though. What's with the pressed jeans and shirt?"

"Traveling clothes. Family requirements. You know how it is."

"Yeah, I guess I do."

"So. Where's this beautiful babe you told me about?"

"Oh, man. She broke my heart. Took up with another dude."

"Already? What happened to, '…this woman, the mother of my children…?"

"Like I said, she took up with some other dude. End of story."

"OK. Don't go ballistic on me."

"Sorry. I'm just a little bit pissed, I guess. I mean, man, she was one fine woman."

"Did you get close to her? Any moonlit walks?"

"Nothing."

"Nothing?"

"I mean nada. We met. We talked. We connected, or so I thought. Next day, when I'm thinking honeymoon, I see her talking and making eyes with some other guy. And, when I walked over, it was like, she never saw me before."

"Go figure, huh?"

"You got that right," he added as they made their way out of the airport to his new 4x4 parked out front."

"Man. Nice set of wheels," Tim said in genuine admiration and envy. "Tell me it's not yours."

"Yeah. It's mine. A little guilt relief present from my old man. I don't see him much since he remarried. He spends all his time with Heather."

"Heather? Your dad married a woman named, Heather?"

"Yeah. Can you believe it? She's probably legal, but I wouldn't bet on it. I've dated women who are old enough to be her mother."

They arrived at the house they would be sharing with four other guys, just as the sun began to slip behind the high mountains. Tim stopped as he got out of the vehicle to watch the daily recurring splendor of nature.

"Awesome."

"I'll say," Karl replied.

"I could never grow tired of looking at those sunsets."

"Sunsets? Who's looking at sunsets? Nature boy, check out the babes coming down the street."

Tim turned reluctantly from the setting sun's display just as two tall blondes walked by without giving a look their direction.

"Have a nice evening, ladies," Karl called after them. "Can you believe that?" he continued. "Not so much as a glance in our direction. Is this how the season is going to go? I may as well just kill myself now. I won't be able to endure if I've lost my magnetism."

Tim had to stifle a laugh as they got his gear out of the vehicle and headed toward the house.

"Come on, Romeo. Magnetism," he chuckled. "Maybe your poles aren't pointing in the right direction. Magnetism," he said again, laughing and shaking his head.

TWENTY-FOUR

The first week of the season was chaotic, to say the least, as Tim struggled to retrain his body to accept the feelings of gliding on waxed slats down the snow-covered inclines. All the hard work in construction helped ultimately, so that by weeks end, he looked like a real pro. By the end of the month, his confidence and ability enabled him to land a job as an instructor. Most of his students were children of rich vacationers who would rather pay than be bothered themselves. They treated him more like a baby sitter than a serious ski instructor he became aware, when he discovered they really weren't interested in their progress reports.

However, unlike many other undertakings, Tim took this quite seriously and he found it rewarding as the children responded and progressed. One chubby little guy in particular was appealing to Tim.

Rodney was ten, had never been on skis and was scared beyond belief. As Tim kneeled to face the boy on eye level, he saw the tears and the doubt as the little guy faced the gentle slope.

"You can do this, Rod." Tim tried to muster all the reassurance he could manage and hide his own doubt.

Sniffing, the boy looked into the eyes of his teacher, searching for hope and help. "I don't think so."

"It's not that far down to the bottom. And just remember one thing, if you feel yourself losing it or beginning to fall, just let go and sit down on your bottom," he recalled the words his friend had said to him not that long ago.

"You sure?" the little guy pled for conviction.
"Absolutely. Just lean forward and give yourself a little push."

"OK." He said with total trust in his new-found friend.

Tim held his breath as the boy began his descent, slowly, very slowly. When the boy didn't fall, Tim raced down the hill to greet his charge at the bottom. Surprisingly Rod made it all the way down the hill without incident – however, he discovered stopping was another unexpected challenge for which there seemed only one solution – crashing full speed into his waiting instructor, sending them both for a spill in the snow.

Finding no damage done, they both laughed when Tim, managing to free himself from underneath the squat boy who weighed almost as much as he did. "I told you, you could do it."

"Yeah. I guess I did," he said with more than a little surprise. "Can we go again?"

"Absolutely!" Tim said, pulling himself and his charge out of the snow. "But, let's work just a bit on stopping."

TWENTY-FIVE

Tim put his entire being into working with the kids he was teaching. However, it was ultimately too much for him, not to mention his little charges, when each of the parents gave him a bored smile of dismissal, or an occasional, "…that's nice," as he attempted to laud the accomplishments of his students.

He seriously considered crumpling the payments he had received and trashing them as he angrily stuffed his belongings into his duffle bag at the end of the season.

"Hey," Karl protested, "don't have a stroke. You did your job. And that's real American legal tender there," he reminded his friend. "Don't get weird on me. You can't change the world."

Tim sat down on the edge of the bed and stared at his friend. "Just tell me one thing."

"What?"

"What's wrong with people?"

"Say again?" Karl looked at him with confusion. "I mean, are you asking me to comment on the over all maladies of humanity, or are we talking specifics here?"

"I don't know, Karl. Are all families that way? Are all parents so preoccupied with their own little worlds that they have no time for their kids? Did you see even one dad on the slopes teaching his kid to ski?"

"Not that I recall. But, don't look a gift horse, etcetera. If Daddy or Mommy had time for little Johnny, you would be several thousand dollars poorer."

"I don't want their damn money," Tim sneered. "It's filthy lucre. It's their guilty conscience balm. And now, I'm part of it. Well, no thank you."

Karl patiently picked up the greenbacks and checks his friend had strewn around the bed and on the floor, stuffing it into an envelope.
"Timmy," he said, in his most patient tone. "You can't change the system, old buddy. As much as you want to, and trust me, it shows all over you – you're a certified reformer at heart. But these people don't want your help, your advice, or your butting into their lives. They come up here to get away from things – from the rat race of their daily existence."

"From their kids?"

"Partly."

"Well, it isn't right. Families are supposed to enjoy each other. They're supposed to want to do things together. These people are missing out and they don't even care."

"Or, they don't know it."

"Excuse me?"

"Maybe you're being just a touch too critical. Just maybe, just maybe, their doing the best they can."

"Well," he responded after a thoughtful pause. "That may be. But they are missing out on some of the most precious moments of their lives. When I saw the look in the eyes of those kids as they managed the seemingly, unmanageable, conquered their fears and built up their own self-confidence, it was just awesome. Totally awesome. And that's what their parents missed out on."

"Yeah, but you were there for them, at least. I saw how those kids looked at you. You should be real proud. You taught those kids to ski. They will most likely remember you for the rest of their lives. You did good Timmy boy," he concluded giving his friend a slap on the back.

"Thanks. I just wish that made me feel better."

"Come on Richmond. It's time to get you to the airport."

As he watched the mountains fall away from view, and the broad expanse of the high plains spread out before him, he vowed to himself and to what ever divine force might be listening that if he ever had kids, it would be different. But, he also realized that Karl was right, and this was the saddest part of all, the parents of those kids didn't even have a clue as to what they were missing.

PART TWO - DONNA

Donna Isom was working alone that Saturday night when Billy Whaley came in the Circle C convenience store. She felt the blood run hot to her face as the flood of memories he caused threatened to drown her. She had never even really talked to Billy. It was his brother who was the cause of her embarrassment all these many years later.

Donna had been a plain girl with few friends and an apparent inability to make more, for some reason. She was a "nice girl", a good student – mostly A's and B's, but she just wasn't popular. Not like the Susie Jones' and Betty Clarks of her ninth grade class at Ft. Collins Junior High. She had tried, for the most part successfully, to leave the past and all of Ft. Collins behind her, but as Billy Whaley strolled around that store in Denver, on a hot summer night, the events of twenty years earlier came back as clearly as if it had been yesterday.

Sitting at a lunchroom table, she was alone, except for the other misfits of her class – Dora Simons, Jean Morris, and Carrie Stump. They weren't really her friends and they didn't talk to her, but she preferred their company to eating her sandwich alone. She usually had a book, which she either read or pretended to read, so no one would think she wanted to talk.

"Hey Donna. What are you reading?"

Startled by the male voice from behind her, one which she recognized immediately, she dropped her sandwich, getting peanut butter and jelly on her dress. In a desperate effort to regain her composure, while suddenly feeling embarrassed as if she were reading something dirty, she put the book in her lap, partly to cover the evidence of the food spill, hoping no one had seen.

Her face was scarlet, she was sure, as she turned and adjusted her thick glasses so she could focus on the face of Jason Whaley, someone who certainly had rarely spoken to Donna though they had been classmates since elementary school.

Jason was one of the tough guys, the object of many early teen crushes and fantasies. Rumors flowed about Jason and the crowd he ran with. They all smoked and probably drank, too. And now, for some unknown reason, Jason Whaley was standing next to her attempting to converse.

"I said, what are you reading?" he repeated.

"Nothing," she swallowed hard to try to get rid of the lump in her throat and the strange squeak in her voice, "Just a book from the library."

Jason sat down in the chair next to her, picking up the book from her lap, exposing the peanut butter and jelly on her dress.

"Better go put some cold water on that jelly. Your Mama won't like you staining that pretty dress. *Little Women*, hum." he said to no one in particular.

"Good book?"

"Yes," she said, really unnerved by this whole scene and hadn't a clue as to what was going on.

"Say, Donna. I was wondering. You got a date for the big dance next weekend?"

She knew her face was going to burst into flame any moment now. "Well," she said, trying to display a modicum of calm and dignity. "I don't think so. Why?"

"Well, I just thought," he said, in the sexiest voice Donna had ever heard except in the movies, as he leaned forward pushing a lock of brown hair back behind her shoulder, "that maybe you would like to go with me. That is if you want to."

That was it. Donna knew without looking that the entire cafeteria was watching – you could have heard a pin drop in the usually deafening room. It was a play, staged for their amusement – at her expense. She was center stage.

"Well, I don't know. I guess that would be all right." Donna was on the verge of tears here as she wanted desperately to flee the arena of her disgrace.

Jason Whaley, seeming totally unaware of her discomfort, grinned and said, "Cool. I'll pick you up about seven."

As he started to get up, Donna thought perhaps she could have been wrong. Maybe he was actually asking her to the dance; though she doubted it. Then the ax fell.

"Oh, by the way, Donna," he said stopping just behind her.

"You will have to 'put-out'."

She stared down at the table in front of her in disbelief as he continued, "Do you 'put-out' much, Donna. You do know what that means, don't you, Donna?"

As he walked away, there came a sudden roar of, was it laughter? Cheering? She could no longer hear clearly and her vision blurred from the tears stinging her eyes. When the bell rang, the students got up and hurriedly left the cafeteria, all except Donna, who sat there with tears dropping from her eyes onto the peanut butter and jelly on her best dress. Her mom would be angry with her.

Billy Whaley, walked up to the register with a swagger identical to what she had seen in his brother so many years before, giving her a look of total non-recognition and said, "Hey, Cutie. How about a pack of smokes – Winston's?"

She turned, wiping her eyes discreetly, picked the pack of cigarettes and returned to her post. "Will that be all?"

"Unless you wanna take a spin in my hot rod with me," he said with a leer, which sickened Donna. Twenty years ago, he might have been attractive, even sexy, like Jason, now he was just disgusting.

"Thanks. But, I guess I'll pass."

"Your loss, Cutie. I could give you a real good time in my hot rod."

Donna froze in her tracks as she looked down with shock and disbelief at the name on the credit card Billy Whaley had just handed her. She knew what to do, she just wasn't sure she could do it.

"Be calm," she told herself, as she fumbled for the silent alarm button. She slid the card through the card reader, waited for a few seconds before she hit Cancel. Then she slid the card again, hoping he wasn't watching too closely.

"I'm sorry," she said with a tremble in her voice she could not control. "The credit card reader must be out of order. I'll have to call the number in for authorization."

Billy Whaley was beginning to show agitation. He had used the card just a few minutes earlier. He knew it worked.

"Well, hurry up, will you. I got places to go."

Donna picked up the telephone and dialed the number on the display above the card reader. Billy couldn't hear what she was saying and didn't know she had dialed a special number to report stolen credit cards. With his back to the door, he also didn't see the Denver Metro Police cruiser pull in to the lot, without its blue lights on – standard response to a silent alarm.

He turned just as two policemen entered the store, casually. Trying to remain calm, he said, "Tell you what. I'll just pay cash for these things. No sense getting the credit card people out of bed."

He stared at the girl in disbelief when the two cops came up on either side of him. One, whom she recognized as Roy, asked, "Is there a problem here Donna?"

"I'm afraid so," she said still trembling handing the credit card to Roy. "That isn't this man's credit card."

"Huh? What are you, crazy? I don't even know you. I never seen you before in my life,"

Billy protested, staring at the woman, wondering, searching his memory. Did he know her? Had he maybe slept with her and forgotten? She did look slightly familiar, though he was sure she wasn't the type he would have dated.

"Sir. May I see some identification," the other officer asked?

"Sure." Billy fumbled in his pocket for the gun he had hoped not to have to pull.

However, he was knocked unconscious by Roy Parks before the gun was fully exposed.

"Donna, you know this guy?" Roy asked after cuffing Billy's hands behind his back.

"His name is Billy Whaley. He comes from Ft. Collins."

The policemen loaded the semi-conscious, groaning man into the back of the cruiser after verifying he was indeed Billy Whaley, who had a string of outstanding arrest warrants, and not the owner of the credit card he had been using.

Roy Parks returned to the store to talk more with Donna Isom about the incident. Had the suspect shown any evidence of threat or violence to her?

"No."

Could she come downtown in the morning to give her statement?

"Yes."

"Donna? Are you going to be okay? Do you need a ride home?"

She liked Roy. He flirted with her when he came in for his free coffee. She forced a smile and said, "I'll be fine. My shift is about over now. My replacement will be here any minute."

TWO

Donna Jean Isom had been the middle daughter in a family of three girls and two older brothers. Her parents were average working-types. Her dad was a mechanic; her mom, a waitress at various Ft. Collins restaurants.

Donna and her sisters Peggy and Betty were expected to clean the house after school and fix dinner for the family. The girls, having decided they didn't mind the work, especially since refusal was out of the question, tried making a game of it and a cooperative effort. The only thing they didn't like about their parents not being home was the teasing and almost abuse they sometimes suffered at the hands of their brothers.

Brad, Jr. and David Isom were less than a year apart in age in a family where the total age spread from oldest to youngest was just over six years. The boys concluded and announced to their sisters, when they were old enough to think about sex, that their old man had finally caught on to where babies came from, or their mom had cut him off. Of course this assumption brought riotous laughter to the brothers and embarrassed giggles to the two oldest girls.

"I don't understand," young Betty would say. "What did Mommy cut off of Daddy's?"

That of course would cause her brothers to howl and she and her sister to blush while trying to change the conversation and usher young Betty out of the room.

"You boys should be ashamed of yourselves," Peggy would say, trying to stifle laughter.

"Oh, we are. Yes ma'am we truly are," they would say in mock sincerity.

Donna actually enjoyed her family life. She didn't like school particularly, though she was a good student. Never a teacher's favorite and in more than one case, she had teachers who did not like her at all.

Her worst experience in school, not counting Jason Whaley, was the year she had spent in Miss Dixon's sixth grade class. Martha Dixon, an unmarried dried-up looking woman of indeterminate age didn't like many of the students in her class, didn't like children in general it seemed, but she obviously hated Donna Isom. The most difficult questions or problems were invariably assigned to Donna.

"No. That's wrong!" she would almost yell. "Sit down."

Donna decided that Miss Dixon was not going to be here undoing, so she began to study harder than she ever had before. Finally, when she was ready for nearly any question or math problem, Miss Dixon just stopped calling on her. So for the rest of the year, when she really didn't know the answer to a question in class, she would simply raise her hand higher, knowing full well that she would be ignored. Donna Isom was finally learning the rules of the game.

THREE

At the age of eighteen, Donna had said goodbye to all of Ft. Collins, leaving only her sister Betty at home with the parents. The joy and laughter had left the Isom home a little at a time with the departure of each of her siblings.

Brad, Jr. had married his teenage sweetheart, Mary Lou, when they graduated from high school. They rented a little apartment across town. Brad, Jr. got a job at the garage where his dad was now the manager and no one seemed to notice or care that little Bobby had been born just six months after they were married. They were as happy as could be, it seemed.

Brother David was obviously his parents' favorite child, something Donna would never understand, since he always seemed to have a cruel streak. At the age of 17, David died in a car accident. Alcohol was involved, of course, and it was unclear who had been actually driving the car at such high speed that it had left the road on a curve, ending the lives of six Ft. Collins teenagers one rainy September evening.

Peggy, who was smarter even than Donna, and a lot prettier, went off to Boulder, to attend the University on a full scholarship. The family showed probably all the enthusiasm and happiness they could manage, having not fully recovered from the loss of David. But everyone was genuinely proud of Peggy and happy for her.

Donna's graduation from high school a year later, on the other hand, was not a pivotal event in anyone's life. They knew she would – and she did. They knew she would move to Denver – and she did that too.

Since she had never liked school, college was not in Donna's plans. All she wanted was to find a good job; rent her own apartment; buy a car, maybe; and that was pretty much the end of her plans. She thought she might like a cat —though she wasn't sure why.

Donna found the jobs were not as abundant or lucrative as she had hoped. She did get a job, a receptionist at an oil company office, since she could type and transcribe dictation. She also had a pleasant telephone voice.

However, on her salary, a car was out of the question and she finally decided a roommate was a necessity. A young girl named Nicki, who worked in an office on another floor of the building, was the first to respond to the notice she had placed on the bulletin board.

The girls seemed compatible. Both from small towns, neither smoked, nor drank, nor even went out much. "I haven't had a date since I got to Denver," Nicki told Donna in quiet confidence one evening.

"Me neither," Donna responded – though in fact, she had gone on very few dates, ever.

All that changed for Donna, however, when Rich Alexander came into her life one morning. He was a courier, delivering packages and messages between businesses and offices in Denver.

"My own idea," he had bragged to Donna on their first unofficial date. "I just decided that there was a need for this type of service in Denver, so I went from business to business, starting first with garages doing parts runs. I now have six guys working for me."

Donna was impressed with Rich's achievements and his overall manner. He was loud, though not in the same way her brothers had been; he was quiet, at times; also, unlike her brothers, who were never quiet. She wasn't sure why she liked him or why he liked her. She still saw herself as an ugly-duckling, ever hoping one day to see a swan in her mirror – that hadn't happened and she was beginning to doubt it would.

Rich and Donna dated for three years, with any talk of marriage – a black cloud hiding their private sun – being avoided. Neither really wanted to get married. For Donna the memories of all the work and responsibility imposed by her parents upon her were still too clear and daunting. She wasn't ready for that again.

For Rich? Well, he wasn't sure why he didn't want to marry Donna. He liked her a lot. He probably, even loved her, he realized. But the very idea of marriage scared the Hell out of him. His parents had divorced when he was thirteen. His dad had been a drunk who slapped him for no reason at all and his mom wasn't much better. Consequently, he spent as much time as possible with his grandmother, who mostly ignored him, playing gin rummy all day with a neighbor and smoking Camel cigarettes.

Rich like being around the woman, though. She never yelled at him, and she certainly never hit him. But he was still afraid of marriage. And even though he didn't even drink at all, he was sure marriage would change everything. Everything changed, anyway, when Donna found herself pregnant.

"Oh, God. How could I let this happen?"

"There. There, Donna." Nicki tried to console her. "It'll be all right. You and Rich can get married. I can find another place to live."

Donna looked at her roommate in disbelief. Sweet-simple Nicki. There wasn't a problem that couldn't be fixed with a simple statement beginning with "It'll be all right."

She hugged the girl and began laughing. Nicki began laughing too, though she wasn't sure why. But she liked the hugging and the laughing. She had come to rely on Donna as her steadying influence in life. She didn't like seeing Donna unhappy or unsure of what to do.

"I doubt that my marrying Rich Alexander will make everything all right. I don't think I even want to marry him and I'm sure he doesn't want to marry anyone."

"But you have to, Donna," Nicki insisted. "It's just not right to have a baby on your own. I mean, a baby is so helpless and so much responsibility. It takes two people to love and care for one."

"Sweet-naïve, Nicki," she said. "This is nineteen hundred and eighty-five. Lots of people have and raise kids alone. Some even do it as a deliberate choice. Besides," she said with a wicked grin, "I've got you to change dirty diapers. Men won't do that."

Nicki gave an uneasy chuckle at her best friend's humor. She wasn't sure she was up to helping raise a baby – but then again, who knew, it could be fun.

"Okay," she said with no further comment.

Donna realizing her friend was uncertain about this whole thing, smiled at her and said,

"Nick. It'll be all right."

FOUR

"Oh, crap! I thought you were using something!"

With that accusatory look and tone, those were not the first words Donna had hoped to hear from Rich when she told him about the situation.

"It was an accident, Rich. They do happen. Your little swimmers managed to breach my little dam."

"I suppose you'll want to get married, now," he added in an almost whining tone.

Donna glared at this man whom she had thought she loved.

"Don't worry about it Rich."

The look of relief in his eyes could not be concealed. "Ah, Honey. You know I'm crazy about you. I'd do anything for you."

"Anything that doesn't involve marriage? Right?"

"Donna, I'll marry you." She looked up, unbelieving, hopefully, for a sign of sincerity in his eyes. Then when he added, "If you want me to," it was too much for her.

"Rich. I don't want to marry you. I wouldn't marry you if you begged me. Now get out of my apartment and leave me alone."

"Ah, Baby. Don't be mad at me." He reached out to embrace her.

"Rich! Get out of here. Now!"

The look on her face told him more than her words. He left without saying anything further, knowing their relationship was over.

Donna dropped on the sofa, allowing herself to sob as she had not since she was a child. Her mind was filled with all the usual questions of a girl in this situation. "How could I have been so stupid? How could I have sex with a man who didn't love me? How could I?"

She fell asleep on the sofa, waking up in a different world – a world with no boy friend, no possibilities for a husband or father for her child – no one, except Nicki, to stand beside her.

Briefly considering the idea of returning to Ft. Collins, she discounted that idea as implausible. She now had to think about her baby and his future. Immediately, she began making plans. She had medical insurance at the company to cover the hospital expenses. She had some money saved, not much, though, most certainly, not enough.

All her calculations and estimations came up to the same conclusions. She simply could not do this on her own, not yet anyway. Donna began to make further plans. First of all Rich was going to have to help her support this baby. It was his obligation and she was prepared to go to court if necessary, she told him when she called him the next week.

"Donna, Honey. You won't have to take ole Richie to court. I'll take care of my kid."

She wondered how many women had heard that promise before? Most likely an awful lot of them. But, for now, she would just have to trust him. When she actually put a number in the conversation, "I figure you can start giving me a hundred a week, then we'll see."

"You mean like now? Donna. The baby ain't even due for another five months. Why do you need the money now?"

"Four months, Rich. The baby, your baby, Rich, is due in four months. There are things to buy. You can't wait till the baby is actually born to get a crib and such. You have to have things ready when you bring a baby home from the hospital."

Donna thought maybe she had misjudged Rich when the following week a delivery truck from a local store showed up at her apartment.

"You Donna Isom?" the man had wanted to know.

"Yes. Why?"

"Sign here please. I got some things for you."

"What kind of things?"

"I don't know lady. Just sign the form then I'll bring them in and you can see for yourself."

There was a room full of boxes when the deliveryman finished. Her first thoughts of gratitude and amazement were momentarily replaced by anger, realizing that Rich had done it all for them instead of with them (she had begun referring to herself as "us" to include her unborn who kicked and moved about so much, she was never unaware of his presence).

Not sure where to start, she just stood staring at all the boxes, when a knock came at the door.

"Someone call for a guy with a screwdriver and a wrench?" he asked when she opened the door.

"Sorry, mister," she said thinking about closing or slamming the door in his face," you must have the wrong address."

But he did look cute in his denim coveralls carrying his little red toolbox. And she certainly didn't know where to start. So, she let him in.

"Rich, you shouldn't have done all this?"

Misunderstanding her meaning, he smiled, saying, "I wanted to."

"That's not what I mean. I wanted to shop for some of this stuff myself."

"Hey, don't be mad at me. I didn't mean to go overboard, or step out of line. I just went into the department store and I guess I went a little crazy. I realized something while I was in the store, it kind of hit me – 'I'm going to be a father.' Is that a scary thought or what?"

She couldn't be mad at him when she saw the look of wonder and amazement come into his eyes when he said that, so she gave him a hug and a kiss on the cheek.

"You know this doesn't change the fact that I don't want to marry you."

"Yeah. Well, maybe one day you will," he said almost hopefully.

They began working on the assortment of boxes, the crib first – which they assembled in Donna's bedroom. She had to admit he had good taste. The crib was white, spindled. And either he knew what he was doing or some saleslady had helped him – and herself to a nice big commission. He had gotten everything – padded bumpers for the crib; a mobile of gingham animals; a small chest of drawers; a little lamp for the chest; a changing table; baby bathtub; a complete layette; and an assortment of stuffed toys.

When they finished, all the empty boxes being carted out, the apartment – especially her bedroom, had been transformed. They were ready for their baby.

FIVE

Richard Connor Isom arrived in the world with a mighty yell on a cold November night. The beautiful almost nine-pound blue-eyed baby boy nursing at her breast and staring up in confused wonder thrilled Donna.

Rich was walking on air. He couldn't believe the event had occurred which would change his life forever after. He had a son. Strutting around at work for the next several days, he was totally unbearable. When he looked at his son, his heart, his whole being melted. He could not believe it.

He also still couldn't comprehend, nor could Donna's mom and dad, that she was refusing to be his wife. He had begged, pleaded, promised her everything, if she would only consent to marry him. Then finally, sadly, he gave up; realizing it was not going to be.

Donna's concession to Rich was to name the baby after him, though she intended to call her baby Connor – a name she had come across in a novel while she was pregnant. He had been little Connor, even before he was born.

He was her joy – she could not remember a time in her life when she was this happy. She sat for days and just stared back into those big blue eyes looking up at her. She began talking to him, telling him things, which he had no way of understanding. And yet the look in those eyes changed over the first few weeks, taking on a knowing, understanding look. The first time he smiled at her, tears streamed down her cheeks.

She worked out an agreeable arrangement with Rich, who came by every day after work to see "His boy." Seeing him sitting and staring at the baby with the same kind of wonder which she had, she smiled to herself. They made quite a picture.

Then, of course, she had to deal with her problem of why she would not agree to marry Rich. She thought perhaps she was being selfish – wanting Connor all to herself. But that couldn't be it, since she was perfectly willing for Rich to come over every day to be with him.

She realized that she didn't trust Rich. His intent seemed genuine enough, but she was fairly certain that he was seeing someone else all the while he was pleading with her to marry him. That was her bottom line – she would not marry someone she could not trust.

Then reality hit when Donna's maternity leave, not to mention her money, ran out. She was faced with the necessity of going back to work, and leaving Connor with someone else, a thought which was repugnant to Donna, Rich and even Nicki.

"What? Leave our baby with a, a stranger," Nicki had protested, stating what they were all thinking. "Little Connor with a stranger? Impossible."

"Look, Donna," Rich had suggested, "If we got married, you wouldn't have to go back to work. I make more than enough money to support us. We could even move out of this little apartment into a house."

At that possibility, the chance to be with Connor and not worry about work, Donna almost caved. "I'll think about it. I really will," she said with a quiet distressing tone that neither Rich nor Nicki had ever heard, nor liked.

SIX

After agonizing over matters for another week, Donna had a plan. That evening when Nicki came home and Rich came by, she told them she had come up with an alternative, hopefully a solution to their problem.

Since, most often, they both depended on Donna to tell them what to do; they stared at her obediently and expectantly.

She began speaking, "Rich, I have grown really fond of you over the past few months. However, I don't think I can marry you. After searching my heart and my feelings, I do not find any romantic love for you, and I feel it would be wrong to marry without that kind of love. While it could develop, I suppose, I don't think it would. Nick, you have become closer to me than any member of my own family has ever been. I care about you the way I would like to have for Peggy and Betty, but they weren't as close and open as you and I have been. Because of my feelings for both of you and hopefully, the feelings you have for each other, here is my proposal. I think we should all move in together – as a family. We can rent a larger apartment or a house and we can all be with Connor and with each other. We can arrange our working hours so that at least one of us is with him at all times. That way, there is no need for any stranger to take care of 'Our little Connor' ever."

Even after she stopped speaking, the other two sat quietly; staring first at the floor; then at each other, then at Donna. They weren't sure they understood or believed the possibilities implicit with her plan – could it really be possible.

Nicki had secretly been afraid that Donna would marry Rich and then move out taking the only true friendship she had ever known along with this wonderful new person in her life, for whom she had already formed such an attachment. She just knew her heart would break if they left.

Rich couldn't believe his ears. Had he heard this woman, the mother of his child, correctly? He thought he really loved her dearly – wanted to be with her and the baby. Could it be that there was a way it could all happen? They both began to smile, a slight small uncertain, hopeful smile, which gave way to huge grins of happiness and anticipation, as the situation and the possibilities began to sink in.

"Let me get this straight," Rich spoke first. "You still won't marry me, but you're willing to live with me?"

"I'm not sure that your living together and my living together mean the same thing – think roommates. We will share the house, the expenses, the cooking, the cleaning."

"The dirty diapers?" Nicki wondered.

"Not me," Rich put in. "I ain't changing no dirty diapers. No sir."

"Okay, Rich," Donna said. "Since you wish to be exempted for dirty diaper detail, what do you propose?"

"Money," he said with a smile. "I have a successful business, so I have more income than the two of you put together. There is no reason you should have to share the cost equally. Hell, I mean heck," he said looking over at the sleeping baby, "I can pay for everything. The two of you can just cook and clean for me – and help take care of my son."

"I'm not sure that would be fair," Donna wondered, though she had to admit she liked the possibility.

"Think about it. If you go back to work, full time, guess who will have to pay for the childcare. Me. Guess who will have to pay for the baby's medical bills. Me. It just makes sense. I'll probably end up saving money over all – and I get to be with the (he started to say two people whom I love most), the son I have grown to love with all my heart."

Donna thought she saw a tear in his eye, which suddenly made her feel guilty and a bit uncertain about this whole arrangement. Was she crazy? Did this have a chance? Time would tell.

SEVEN

One Saturday morning in late April, Rich announced at breakfast that he wanted to take everyone for a ride after they ate.

"Ride? To where?" Donna seemed suspicious.

"Just never you mind. It's a surprise."

After the meal was finished and the kitchen cleaned up, they all piled in to Rich's new pickup and headed across town. He drove them in to a residential area, which appeared to be a fairly well maintained working class area. The houses were mostly frame with an occasional small brick home. The lawns were manicured and the landscaping was good – all signs of a stable neighborhood. After several twists and turns, at which time Donna realized she was completely turned around and could not get out if she had to, Rich pulled into the driveway of a nice looking white two story house. Though it defied categorizing – it wasn't Colonial and yet it had Colonial touches – it was appealing with its huge front porch and large windows.

A real estate sign in the front yard displaying a "SOLD" sign, told Donna this was going to be their future home. She liked the fact that Rich was a take charge kind of person, and yet she resented the fact that he did, and bought things without consulting the others involved.

"Ladies," Rich said rather grandly. "Welcome to your new home."

"Rich. How could you?" Donna wanted to know.

"Donna. It's his money after all," Nicki chided. "Can't you show a little gratitude for once?"

With those remarks, Donna realized she had gone too far. The hurt look on Rich's face and the look of dismay on Nicki spoke volumes. She looked at Rich and said, "I'm sorry. She's right. It is your money. I'm sure we will all love it."

"If not, we send it back," Rich responded with a half-smile.

As it turned out, the house was great. They all loved it, especially the back yard.

"Oh. This is going to be a wonderful place for our little Connor to play," Nicki said.

Donna tried to apologize to Rich, but it seemed like it was a half-hearted effort at best. She still felt she was right – that something, which affected them all so greatly, should have been a decision of mutual agreement. Obviously Rich did not see her reasoning and apparently Nicki didn't either.

The living arrangement actually seemed to work well. Nicki and Rich had jobs during the day, when Donna was at home with Connor. Then when Donna started working at nights as a night manager for Circle C Convenience Stores, Rich and Nicki were home. Everybody seemed happy and Connor was thriving.

EIGHT

After two years of pursuit and rejection, Rich seemed to despair of winning Donna's consent to marry. She just couldn't quite convince herself that he was serious. She knew he loved Connor, beyond belief and he was a good father.

He was more than generous in the things he was willing to do and provide for their, albeit unusual, family arrangement. She told herself it should be enough. She should jump at the chance to marry Rich. But something wasn't right. She couldn't put her finger on it, but she knew there was something.

In the week prior to Connor's third birthday, Donna had seemed to pickup a virus. Her head had been pounding and she was running a fever on Wednesday night, so she told the woman working with her that she was going home early, though she had only been at work for two hours when she left.

Everything seemed quiet, too quiet in the house when she arrived at just after nine-thirty. The house was clean, nothing was out of place. Both Rich's and Nicki's cars were in the drive, so she reasoned they were both at home, probably reading or watching TV in their rooms. She stopped upstairs on her way to her room, looking in on Connor who was peacefully sleeping in his crib. She left the room quietly, heading toward her room next to the nursery, when she heard a noise coming from Rich's bedroom.

She froze in her tracks when she noticed that Nicki's door was open and the room was not occupied. She didn't know what to do next. Should she go to her room, pretending not to notice or should she leave the house quietly, returning at her regularly scheduled time.

Her decision was made for her when the door to Rich's room opened and her two best friends came into the hallway wearing robes and heading toward the bathroom.

"Oh my God!" Donna could not believe what she was seeing.

"Donna," Nicki said in shocked disbelief.

"Well aren't you two the pretty pair," she said turning and entering her own room.

She couldn't believe what she had seen and yet she should have suspected it. She felt certain this was not a first-time event or even a short-term affair. Things had just seemed different for about the past year.

Rich had stopped even asking her to marry him and Nicki, who had been very quiet and soft spoken in the beginning, had become very critical of Donna.

"Donna," it was Rich at her door. "May I come in?"

"It's your house," she responded sarcastically. "Apparently you can do whatever you wish – or whoever you wish."

"Donna, it isn't like that. Nicki and I have fallen in love. We didn't plan it. It just happened. At first she felt sorry for me, because you wouldn't marry me. Then something else developed."

"And I guess her way of showing her sympathy was to have sex with you?"

"Look, Donna. I know you're mad. I don't blame you. But we weren't trying to deceive you and, God knows, we didn't want to hurt you. We both love you."

"And are you now planning to marry Nicki?"

"We have discussed marriage. But nothing has to change. We can still be a family."

"A family? Rich, are you crazy. This changes everything. I will take my son and find another place to live."

"Donna. Connor is my son, too. And Nicki loves him as well. You can't just take him and move. We can fix this. I know it."

"No, Rich, I don't think we can. I don't have a mayonnaise jar."

"A what?"

"When I was little, actually all my life, my mother kept a mayonnaise jar under the kitchen sink. Whenever she or anyone else found a button, a missing piece to a game or puzzle, a screw, anything loose, it went into the jar. Then when someone was looking for a missing piece, they usually found it there. Well, Rich, something is definitely lost here now and I don't have a mayonnaise jar to look in for the missing pieces."

"But you can't do this. You can't just take Connor and leave."

"And why can't I."

"Because I got rights. I'm the father here, Donna."

"Well, I think you should have thought about that before you slept with the nanny."

"That's not fair."

"Maybe not, but that's life. Now if you will excuse me, I'm not feeling very well and I want to rest."

Rich turned and left the room, closing the door quietly behind him. He knew she was probably right. And he never should have slept with Nicki. He would probably never love anyone the way he loved Donna. He just shook his head as he went into his room and lay across his bed.

Donna wasn't sure why she was so upset. They were adults, after all, and these sorts of things do happen. If Rich and Nicki were truly in love, why couldn't she be happy for them? It just seemed that the two people closest to her had violated a trust, an unwritten code. Rich had obviously been having sex with Nicki before he stopped asking – begging her to marry him. She wasn't sure what that said about his commitment to Nicki, if indeed he had made any, but she knew what it meant to her – she still could not trust the one person she wanted to trust, needed to trust – the man she loved. No, she couldn't fix this even if she had a mayonnaise jar, because the missing piece would never be in a jar, it could only be found inside a heart. Obviously, that missing part was not in Rich's heart and she could not put it there.

NINE

Once again, Donna briefly considered returning to Ft. Collins, taking her son and moving back in with her parents. But she knew it would not work, so she found an apartment not too far away from the house – strange how she felt an outsider, again. She had really never felt totally at home in the house. It was Rich and Nicki's house. It had always been their house no part of it was ever Donna's.

She looked for someone to take care of Connor while she was working. However, the economics of the situation forced her to face reality. So each evening, on her way to work, she would drop Connor off at "the house" and pick him up after. Every other weekend, Rich would come by and pick Connor up for the day.

Rich and Nicki broke off their relationship, or never resumed it after that evening. Shortly after Donna left, Nicki moved out also. She could not face Donna nor could she and Rich face each other knowing the guilt they bore for breaking up the family. They had violated the rules and deserved what ever followed. Banishment seemed the only appropriate punishment for Nicki.

Donna soon developed a routine and began to enjoy her time with her son as much as ever – only rarely did the vague sense of loss and longing for something more make her yearn for the happy times she had known with Rich and Nicki. She did not, however, dwell on these feelings, reminding herself, it was they, not she, who had broken the rules.

As the weeks turned into months – months into years, Donna came to terms with the missing part of her life – a physical and more importantly an emotional relationship with someone she loved and trusted. As he grew and flourished, Connor became the central focus of her existence. Only on rare occasions did she long for the feel of a lover's breath on her neck or the touch of a hand on her bare skin. When it would happen, she would shake her head or shrug off the longing and move on with her day; with her life. However, when Billy Whaley and Timothy Addison entered her life, she was so totally and visibly shaken that she turned to Rich for comfort and security.

"Donna," Rich implored. "Why won't you take me back? How long is it going to take for me to prove my love to you?"

"Rich. You don't have to prove anything to me. I'm not asking you to. I know you love me."

"Then why can't we be together?"

"We are together, aren't we?"

"You know what I mean. I want us to be together all the time. Not just when you get shaken and realize you need someone to lean on. Dammit, Donna. I've never loved anyone the way I love you."

"I know that Rich," she admitted, kissing him tenderly. "Maybe one day that will be enough."

He knew what she meant and fell silent, holding the true love of his life close to him, wondering what was wrong with him? Wondering why he couldn't make it in a normal one-on-one relationship? As he gazed out the window at the black Colorado sky, he doubted he would ever find the missing key that would unlock that doorway and allow him to pass through. He sighed knowing full well that as sure as he was that he wished it not to be so, he would find himself in some smoky bar, a restaurant or just walking down the street when someone would flash him that invitational look and he would follow. He didn't know why, he just knew he would.

PART THREE

Mark Addison did not call Eric the day of the visit to Police HQ, or the next, or the day after that. He also did not return to work the following Monday. Instead he contacted a service arranging for a fill-in to take care of his patients until he could make some sense of things.

With the help of a private investigator obtained by his attorney, they were piecing together a picture of Tim's activities after leaving Richmond almost a month earlier. Credit card records indicated he traveled south out of Virginia on Interstate 81, purchasing gas and food in the small town of Abingdon, near the Tennessee border.

He had then proceeded into Tennessee, picking up Interstate 40 west, making a stop in Knoxville. From that point on, everything was pretty much the same. Stop in Memphis, Ft. Smith Arkansas, Amarillo, TX, then Taos, NM.

He was apparently not calling anyone along the way, as there were nothing recorded on his new cell phone. In addition, he was obviously sleeping along the highway – probably at rest areas, as there were no motel charges.

In Taos, after several days with no activity, he purchased some sort of jewelry at a gift shop. The cost of the item or items was $78. Tim was not known to wear rings or chains, so this seemed to be an odd occurrence to his brother.

After those charges, there were several other purchases, including gas in Denver. The next bit of unwelcome information caused Mark's head to spin and a cold chill ran down his spine.

The record showed, *Attempted use of the card by an unauthorized user reported – account closed.*

No further activity was reported. The private investigator, whose name was Sam, tried to sound reassuring when he said, "This doesn't necessarily mean anything, Doc. He could have just lost the card."

"Then exactly what do you think he would have been using for gas and food over the next two weeks. He didn't take a lot of cash and there was no money in his bank account to access."

"But, it still doesn't necessarily suggest foul play."

"Then what does it suggest?"

Mark left the attorney's office – he had to get some air. As he went out the door, he heard the attorney tell Sam, "Call the Denver police. See what they know about this."

Sam Jennings, a short-stocky man in his late fifties, had been a private investigator all his life. However, he had mostly done surveillance of individuals involved in lawsuits and divorces. But, along the way, he had developed a sort of sixth sense about things. Something was telling him that Tim Addison had indeed met up with bad hombres on his visit to the western mountains. He didn't want to impart that feeling to the Doctor however, as he could see the guy was barely holding himself together.

He made two calls to the Denver Police Department; neither attempt was successful in obtaining the information he wanted. However, on the second call, the officer directed him to Sgt. O'Riley, Missing Persons' Unit, Richmond PD.

"So," he thought to himself as he headed downtown toward police headquarters, "Our own city's finest is already on this case." He wanted to find out what this Sgt. O'Riley knew or had that he didn't, naturally, without revealing what he knew.

He arrived at the office of Missing Persons' at precisely nine-thirty. At ten-forty, a pleasant looking young woman approached him, "Mr. Jennings?"

"Yes? I'm Sam Jennings."

"Mary O'Riley, Mr. Jennings. What can I do for you?"

"Please call me Sam. I want to talk with you about Timothy Addison."

"Come this way, please."

After showing him into a small cubicle at the back of the room and closing the door, she asked, "What do you know about Timothy Addison?"

"Not a whole lot, I'm afraid. I was hoping maybe you could enlighten me."

"What is your connection?"

"I'm sorry," he said offering her his card. "I'm a licensed Private Investigator, retained on behalf of the family. I am trying to find Tim Addison, the same as you. Therefore, I was hoping that, perhaps we could help one another."

He sensed Mary O'Riley bristle slightly at the implication that she or her department would require any assistance in this investigation. However, she forced a benign smile, and asked, "Exactly what sort of assistance are you prepared to offer the Department?"

Sam could see that this visit was most likely a wasted effort. This woman was sharp and she was going to play her cards very close to the vest.

"I'll be perfectly frank with you. Is it Miss O'Riley, or do you prefer Ms.?"

"Sgt. O'Riley will do, thank you, Mr. Jennings."

Sam was beginning to wonder if she disliked all men or had he just alienated the crap out of her within the first two seconds of their meeting. He was perfectly capable of doing just that, he realized all too well. Deciding to try a different tack, Sam became apologetic and almost unctuous, saying, "I'm terribly sorry, Sgt. O'Riley. I guess this isn't a good day. Perhaps I should come back another time."

As he was standing, Mary O'Riley smiled, slightly, and said, "Sit down, Sam. I guess I'm just a little overly sensitive and overworked these days."

"No problem Sgt. O'Riley." Sam sat back down with a huge self-congratulatory smile.

"Now, as I was saying, I have been retained on behalf of the family of Tim Addison. We have gotten up to date phone and credit card receipts which show that Tim was headed toward Colorado."

He knew that she would have gotten the charge information so he wasn't telling her anything she didn't know – but he hoped she didn't know that he knew.

"It appears his actual last charges were made in Taos, New Mexico, however. An attempted use of his card in Colorado, by an unauthorized user ended in the arrest of that person, apparently after the card had been either lost or removed from his person."

Sam Jennings paused at this point hoping that Mary O'Riley would pick up the line of discussion and tell him what she knew beyond that point. Instead, she waited for a moment also, before asking, "Have you been in contact with the Denver Police?"

"I made a call, but I was unable to speak with anyone who could offer any assistance." This was only partially untrue.

"I have talked with Denver on several occasions. They have an individual in custody for the Credit Card offense. However, they do not feel he is directly connected to the disappearance of Tim Addison."

Now she was talking. Sam hoped with a little friendly coaxing she would continue.

"Do you mind if I take my jacket off?" he asked, slipping the out-of-season blazer off his shoulders.

Mary then decided to make a gesture of friendship. Who knew, this strange little man might be able to help her case.

"Would you like some coffee, Sam?"

"I'd love a cup, Sgt."

While she was gone from the room, he tried reading her file notes upside down, something he had become accomplished at over the years, committing the details and the names Billy Whaley, Donna Isom and Circle C to memory, in case she didn't volunteer any names or other information.

Mary returned with two steaming Styrofoam cups of coffee. Sam hated Styrofoam cups, but he took the one extended to him and said, "Thank you, very much."

"Now where were we?" Mary asked seeming totally relaxed now, which surprised Sam.

"We were in Denver."

"Yes. Well, unfortunately, that's where the trail ends, for us, at least."

"I'll admit, I don't know a whole lot more than you. We are making efforts to have someone interview this Whaley character and Ms. Isom." He dropped the names hoping she would think that he had known them all along.

Mary glanced down at her open file trying to determine if it had been moved in her absence. Everything seemed in order, so she gave him a little credit for not being a total snoop. If he could read upside down, that was one thing. Flipping through her file was another.

"We are also making a list of acquaintances of Tim Addison in an effort to find any common links to the New Mexico, Colorado area," he added.

"I think we have already checked all those people out," Mary stated.

"Did you find an old college classmate who had moved to Denver last year?" Sam was grasping at straws here.

"I don't think so? I don't recall any such person? Do you have a name?"

"Not at this point. Something was mentioned in one of my conversations with the family." He tried to sound convincing in this lie. "I'll let you know if we come up with the name."

"You do that," Mary was now aware that this guy had nothing to offer. Deciding to end the meeting, she stood up abruptly. "Well, Sam. I'm sorry, but I have another appointment. It was very nice meeting you."

"You too, Sgt. O'Riley."

TWO

Donna Isom had already talked to the Denver Police more times than she cared to remember, so when the two men approached her on that Friday evening, it was almost the final straw.

"Look. I already told the police, I don't know anything except that this creep came into the store; tried to pay for his things with a stolen credit card; I sounded the alarm; the police came and arrested him. End of story."

"Please, Miss Isom," Sam Jennings implored. "How did you know the card was stolen? Had you met Tim Addison or perhaps seen him in the store?" Sam knew there were no other charges at the Circle C, but he was pushing to see if there was something she wasn't telling – he felt certain there was.

Donna didn't like the little man in the rumpled raincoat. He was really starting to tick her off, big time.

"I never heard of Tim Addison. I wouldn't have even remembered the name if the cops hadn't asked about it so many times. I'm beginning to wish I had just let the creep use the card and leave."

"Miss Isom," Mark Addison spoke up for the first time – contrary to the wishes of Sam Jennings, who has insisted, '...Let me do the talkin', Doc.' "I'm very sorry that we have taken up so much of your time, but this is extremely important."

She looked at the other man who had not said anything other than hello, when they first arrived. He had a sadness in his eyes which she could not ignore.

"What's your angle here?" she wanted to know.

"Angle?" Mark seemed puzzled at the use of that word. "I assure you I have no angle. Tim Addison is my brother, that's why I'm here."

"Sorry. I really don't think I can help you though. I knew who Billy Whaley was because he comes from my hometown. That's it. There is nothing more to tell."

"Did he offer any comments or explanations when the police were questioning him about how he got the card? Did he say he borrowed it? Or that it was loaned to him?"

"No. That's the strange thing about it – that's what I expected him to do. Instead, when the one cop asks him for some ID, he tries to pull a gun and the other cop whacks him one. He's just a stupid jerk."

"Would you take a look at this photo of Tim," Mark asked. "Do you think you may have ever seen him?"

"I already saw this picture. The cops have it. And my answer is still the same – no. I never saw him before that I remember. The cops took all our video tape for the past two weeks, trying to spot his face. That's really all I know. Look, I have to get back to work. I don't want to lose my job just because I was awake that night."

She followed the two men out of the back office, through the store and out the door to the dreary August, Denver day. There was a nip in the air and rain had been falling steadily since early morning. Fall was coming to the Rockies.

Mark Addison turned up his collar and put his wool racing cap on his head, the whole thing – the weather, this city, this situation – sent a chill down his neck and spine. He had thought coming to Denver would help, but he was beginning to feel there was nothing here.

"We may as well go back to Richmond," Mark had said to Sam.

"Not so fast, Doc. First we go to the Police Station to talk to Billy Whaley for ourselves."

THREE

Denver Metropolitan Police Headquarters, a one-block square modern three story building, was totally opposite from Richmond PD. The building and offices were spacious, well lit and airy, for which Mark Addison was grateful. He would never forget the feeling he had gotten in the small airless cubicle he and his brother had shared with Mary O'Riley.

Sgt. Arnold, a pleasant enough guy, was the officer in charge of the Timothy Addison, missing person, file – though he really didn't have much of a file.

"What can I do for you fellows?" he wanted to know.

"We want to talk to you about the Timothy Addison case and any possible connection with a felon by the name of Billy Whaley.

After determining that they were Tim's next of kin and a private investigator hired by the family, he led them back to a private room where they could talk.

"To be perfectly honest gentlemen. Denver PD doesn't really have much of a case. We have nothing to indicate Timothy Addison was ever in Denver. I think Colorado State Patrol is coordinating this with Richmond, VA. As for Billy Whaley, there was nothing really except several convictions for other minor offenses and this charge for attempted theft by credit card, which is a misdemeanor."

"Can we talk to him?" Mark Addison wanted to know.

"If you can find him."

"What does that mean?"

"He was released on Bail pending his hearing – for which he didn't show. But we really don't think he is a suspect in the disappearance of Mr. Addison."

"And exactly why is that?" Sam was trying to take charge.

"Well, like I said. Whaley is a small-time hood. There is nothing in his file which is a felony, except one marijuana possession wrap."

"How did he explain having the credit card?"

"Says he found it. My guess is he probably bought it for a few dollars from someone else. It happens all the time."

"But there is absolutely nothing to link him to Tim Addison?"

"Not so far as we can tell. As I said before, we have no reason to believe Tim Addison was ever in Denver. Whaley doesn't live in Denver; he was just passing through, when he tried to use someone else's credit card."

"What about the car?" Mark wanted to know.

"What car?"

"The car he was driving – the one which your guys would have impounded. What kind of a car was it?"

"Don't think there was one. There's nothing in the report about a vehicle being impounded. I guess he was on foot."

"In that neighborhood? Didn't look like the sort of area a person would be on foot."

Sam was impressed, and a little jealous. Mark Addison had come up with something that had not even occurred to him and obviously had not occurred to the police.

"We'll check it out. But like I say, we really don't have much to go on."

Sam and Mark Addison thanked the officer for his time and left the station heading back across town.

FOUR

They arrived at the home of Donna Isom, using the address she had given them when Mark called.

"Come in Dr. Addison. Mr. Jennings. I really don't think I have any more information for you, but I'll be glad to listen."

"We have just been to the Police Department. Whaley has jumped bail and is nowhere to be found."

"Somehow that doesn't surprise me."

"But there is one thing of interest that we did learn. The police think Whaley was on foot when he arrived at the store. Do you have any recollection of that?"

"Not really. I didn't notice him till he was in the store. But we don't get much foot traffic at that location." she paused. "But, there is a way to find out."

"How?"

"The store has an outside surveillance camera. Unless it was turned off, which it is never supposed to be, we should have a tape."

"I thought the police had the tapes."

"They only took the inside camera recordings."

"When can we look at those tapes?" Sam asked since he was really feeling ignored – this was his line of work.

"I go to work at five. After I pick my son up from school, I could meet you there. I'll call the owner and tell him what we need to do – there shouldn't be any problem."

They met Donna at the Circle C just after four-thirty. They exchanged the usual greetings and went inside the store.

"Hey Donna," called the cashier working at the register.

"Hi Pam. Listen, I may need you to work a little late today. Would that be okay?"

"Okay by me. I need the money."

"Great. Thanks."

She led the men back to the store office and opened the fire-proof safe where the videos were kept.

"We keep these tapes for several years, just in case someone wants to try to sue us for a slip and fall or other incident – amazing how much a person's memory improves after they see the tapes. This should be it," she said selecting a tape and putting it in the machine. After a few minutes of fast-forward they came to an on-tape meter-reading of 20:35. "This should be just a few minutes before he came into the store."

"There is a vehicle pulling in now," Sam announced.

"Oh my God!" Mark Addison felt ill at the sight of the gray and green Ford Bronco stopping in front of the door. He sank back in his chair, not wanting to believe what he was seeing. The others were looking at him, knowing what he was going to say, "That's Tim's car."

They watched the video for several more minutes. They saw a Denver Police cruiser pull in next to the Bronco. Then an interesting thing occurred, the driver of the Bronco – not Billy Whaley, calmly backed out of the parking space and left the lot.

"I can't believe this," Sam uttered.

FIVE

The three of them sat at the table with Sgt. Arnold as the video player repeated the scene – the green and gray Bronco pulls up to the store. The driver, a man who is partly obscured from view, stays in the vehicle. Billy Whaley gets out on the passenger side and struts into the Circle C. Minutes pass while the driver sits in the car, smoking and looking around, the Denver Metro Police cruiser pulls up. The officers get out of the car and go in the store. The Bronco driver, appearing in no particular hurry, backs away from the building and drives off. Several minutes later the police exit the building escorting a handcuffed Whaley to the back of the cruiser – the cruiser pulls away from the building.

"Why weren't we told about this tape earlier?" Sgt. Arnold seemed to want to place responsibility for this oversight on someone other than Denver PD.

Donna spoke up in answer. "I guess all the police asked for were the in-store tapes, and then only because they wanted to see if Tim Addison had been in the store. They weren't concerned about who was on the parking lot."

"Well, Sgt.," Sam Jennings asked, "does this change Denver's involvement in this case."

"Unless the driver of the vehicle was actually Tim Addison, it would appear that a stolen vehicle was used in commission of another crime in the city. Yes. That would change our involvement in the case."

"I assure you that was not my brother driving the Bronco," Mark said.

"How can you be sure? You couldn't see his face."

Mark was more than a little annoyed by the police officer's comment, but decided to just answer his question.

"Number one, my brother doesn't smoke – he can't even stand to be around anyone who does. Number two, the man in the car was obviously much heavier than my brother – Tim weighs in at about one-sixty. Number three, unless he shaved and got a hair cut, Tim has a full beard and long hair. Number four, it would be rather asinine for him to send someone else in to use his credit card to purchase things. Number five, why would he drive away, leaving his buddy, when the police came? If for some reason, he had sent the guy in with his card, there was no crime."

"I guess you make a good case," Sgt. Arnold conceded. "We'll put out a bulletin for a stolen vehicle on the green and gray Bronco and we will issue another arrest warrant for Billy Whaley. Is there anything else that any of you detectives have to offer?" he said with a bit too much sarcasm.

"No. But if we do come up with anything else, we'll let you know," Sam Jennings responded in kind.

"Please do that," the officer said.

SIX

Mark Addison slept in short fitful stretches that night. Pounding the pillow for the umpteenth time, he cursed and decided to get up and shower. The clock said it was only four-thirty.

In his dreams, he kept seeing the green and gray Bronco pull into the parking lot of the Circle C convenience store. The obscured face of the driver along with that of Billy Whaley would come into view laughing, leering at him like macabre clowns. Then he would see his brother's lifeless form discarded along the highway, like so much refuse. He put on jeans, a shirt, and his coat, then went outside into the cold damp dreary Denver early morning. There was little traffic moving and fewer signs of life otherwise. The hotel restaurant was still closed. However he saw a sign, "OPEN 24 HOURS" not far away.

Heading in that direction, he hoped the sign was connected to an establishment with coffee, at least, if not real food. He was extremely hungry. As he rounded the corner of the building, turning his collar up against the blast of cold air and rain, he was rewarded with the sight of a Waffle House coming into view.

Stopping first for a copy of the *Denver Post*, he entered the restaurant greeted by a blast of heat and noise almost as suddenly and hard as the wind and rain had earlier. This time, however, it was laughter, raised voices, a blue haze of cigarette smoke, and the loudest jukebox he had ever heard that assaulted him. Doubting the wisdom of his actions and whether he could endure this atmosphere long enough to eat, he found the one unoccupied booth at the rear and sat down.

A waitress appeared out of nowhere with a steaming pot of black liquid. "Coffee?" was her only greeting.

"Sure."

"Cream?"

"No," he said uncertainly. "Black is fine."

"Menu's over there." And with that she left him to his paper and cup of coffee.

He scanned the headlines as he took his first tentative sip of the dark liquid in his cup. He had honestly never seen coffee that black. But it was drinkable and it was strong – which he needed. Upon reaching the second page of the paper, a small article caught his eye immediately:

> New Evidence in Disappearance
> **Of Richmond, VA Man**
> ***Metro Police Sgt. Thomas Arnold***
> informs that additional information
> has developed in the disappearance
> of Timothy Addison of Virginia.
> Sgt. Arnold said that Addison's
> apparently stolen vehicle had been
> observed on video-tape from the
> Circle C store where an attempted use
> of his credit card resulted in the arrest
> of one man. No other details were
> available to us at press-time.

Mark wasn't much of a breakfast person, but he thought he was hungry this morning, most likely because of lack of sleep. He ordered eggs and toast, returning to his paper and coffee after the waitress left.

He ate without really tasting the food. His mind was preoccupied with the events of the previous days and weeks, trying to decide what the next logical moved might be. He concluded that they had accomplished all they could hope for in Denver and decided to fly back to Richmond

SEVEN

Mary O'Riley had spent a minimum of twelve hours a day at her desk since the photo of Tim Addison had landed there a month earlier. She was getting nowhere on her end and Colorado Police weren't getting much further. Tim's brother Mark and Sam Jennings had given Denver the only conclusive evidence they had that a crime had been committed in the area – though not necessarily in Denver, Sgt. Arnold had been quick to interject.

She had spent countless hours poring over John Doe morgue photos which had come in by the dozens from New Mexico, Texas, Oklahoma, Colorado and Wyoming. All the photos that bore any resemblance to Tim Addison because of apparent age or height and weight were placed in a separate folder for review with the brothers. Mark Addison was due in her office within the hour to discuss any new developments and to look at the latest batch of photos. Eric Addison, it seemed had lost interest in his brother's routine, making the excuse that he could not afford to leave his practice.

The latest shipment of information on John Doe patients at hospitals in the five-state region were also on her desk awaiting attention. Some had photos, most had just descriptions. She met Mark Addison in the reception area and suggested they take their stacks of work to the employee lounge downstairs, sensing that the interview room was a little too close for the doctor. He seemed greatly pleased by the suggestion.

"Anything new out of Denver?" Mark asked on the elevator.

"Not really," she responded as they left the car.

"I just can't understand why they haven't found the vehicle yet?"

"It's a fairly common vehicle type and the pair probably aren't even in Colorado anymore. They could be in California or Canada or Mexico, by now."

"What other new things do you have? More photos?"

"Yes. Some are rather…"

"I know."

They sipped hot coffee and looked at the morgue photos. Funny, Mark thought, how different people look after death. The features, the coloring, everything changes rapidly. He had always been amazed at the miracle of life, anyway. Such a fragile existence was life. Almost like a candle flame, so easily extinguished by the slightest breeze. And yet people, including some of his patients, clung so tenaciously to life, it was remarkable. That learned scholars, mystified, unable to explain life's very existence, were willing to accept, even embrace the theory of a chaotic beginning to life had always amazed him. Mark had never had a problem with the concept of God and the more he learned, by observation and study, the more convinced he became that no other explanation for the beginning of life made sense.

More than an hour later, the pile of photos and reports having proved fruitless, Mark Addison stood, sighing as he tossed the last one back on the heap.

"Don't give up," she encouraged. "There will be more tomorrow.

"And the tomorrow after that, and the one after that," he responded. "I'm beginning to think this is all useless. It's like looking for the proverbial needle."

"I know it seems hopeless. But, we have to keep looking."

Mark turned in surprise at the insistence and urgency in her voice. He smiled at the officer. "Isn't that supposed to be my job? Begging you to keep looking?"

"Sorry," she responded with genuine embarrassment. "I tend to get a little bit involved, sometimes."

"Thanks," Mark said touching her hand. "I appreciate the pep talk. I'll see you when you get some more photos."

EIGHT

Later that week, Mary O'Riley was reading over the reports from the rural county hospitals in Wyoming when she stopped.

"Oh, God," she uttered, picking up the phone and dialing.

"I may have found something," she said after his hello.

"I'll be right there."

"Listen to this," She said in greeting half and hour later.

"Male, six-one, brown hair and beard, brown eyes, no distinguishing body marks. Comatose, suffering severe head trauma, admitted July 29th, this year."

"That could be Tim – where is that from?"

"Albany county hospital near Cheyenne, Wyoming, it's not that far out of Colorado, really." She was on the telephone already.

"No photo?"

"No," she said as she finished dialing the number. An operator came on at the hospital. "Hello? Yes, this is Sgt. Mary O'Riley from the Richmond, Va., Police Department. I need to speak to your director of nursing services, please."

There was a brief pause, which seemed interminable to Mark who appeared to be not breathing, as the original message was repeated. Followed by, "…is the patient still there?"

"Fine. I think there is a possibility this may be a Richmond, VA man who has been missing. Do you have a fax machine? I would like to fax you his picture. Great. Thanks."

Mark could no longer hear and his vision had almost narrowed to pinpoints. He realized if he didn't get some oxygen in his system he was going to pass out. He sipped at some water and tried some deep breathing hoping to rectify the situation.

Mary O'Riley left the office on the run and was back at the desk within a few minutes. Mark's trauma had abated by then. They sat staring at each other, hardly breathing not speaking, not daring to hope they had found Tim – and yet they both prayed it would be so. It seemed an hour passed before the telephone's ringing startled them both.

"Mary O'Riley?" she answered into the receiver. "Yes. Yes. I understand. Thank you."

"What was it?" Mark Addison wanted to know.

"They can't tell. The patient has been heavily bandaged because of the injury and the surgery."

"Can't they try something else? Fingerprints? Something?"

"They've already shipped the prints to the FBI for comparison. However, since your brother was never arrested, and never served in the military, his prints may not be on file."

"How about DNA, or dental records. My brother Eric has a complete set of his dental records."

"That's fine, but keep in mind, this man was seriously injured. They may not be able to examine his teeth."

"Why is he still in a small county hospital? Why haven't they moved him to a larger facility?"

"John Doe's don't get priority treatment. His condition did not warrant that."

"Well, I'm catching the next plane to Wyoming." he said rising from his chair.

"It may be a wasted trip," she cautioned.

"I can't just sit here. I have to see for myself."

"Would you like me to make a call? I can probably get you some VIP treatment – if it's necessary."

"I don't care. I'm going home and pack a few things."

"Call me. Please."

He looked at Mary O'Riley, genuinely moved by the fact that his brother was not just another case to her. As her supervisors had said, "Mary gets too involved in her cases…"

NINE

When the Frontier Airlines jet made its approach for landing in Cheyenne, Mark was surprised to see snow on the tops of the highest mountains in the distance. When the cold air outside hit him, he was no longer surprised.

Leaving the jetway, and focusing on the airport terminal, he was planning to find the nearest phone and call his wife, when an official looking person approached him.

"Excuse me, sir. Are you Dr. Addison?"

"Yes. I'm Mark Addison."

"Dr. Addison, I'm Dave Stone with the FBI. We got a call from Richmond, VA Police that you were coming out on a missing person's case. I am the local officer for the Bureau. I was asked to pick you up and transport you to the hospital and help in any way I can."

"That's very generous of you Mr. Stone."

"Dave. Please call me Dave."

"Okay. I want to go to the hospital first. After that, I suppose that I need to find a place to stay."

"That's all been taken care of Dr. Addison. You can stay at the hospital as long as you want. Either I or my assistant will be able to help you at any time."

The ride to the hospital took about thirty minutes. In spite of his concern and anticipation, Mark could not help but admire the beauty of the countryside and the deep blue of the sky. You don't see much blue sky in Richmond anymore, he thought sadly to himself.

Seeming to be reading his thoughts, Dave Stone asked, "This your first trip to Wyoming, Dr. Addison?"

"Yes. And I was just thinking about how beautiful it is here."

"I grew up here. After the military took me to the far reaches of the earth, I decided this was the most beautiful spot I had seen, so I moved back."

"I think that's understandable."

They arrived at the hospital and after parking the vehicle, they walked in to the building. The familiar antiseptic smell welcomed Mark Addison and for a moment he thought he was making rounds or just checking on a patient.

They were directed to the nurses' station on second floor, where they met the nurse in charge of the John Doe patient in 4W. "He was admitted on July 29$_{th}$," she began reading the chart to the doctor. "His head injuries do not seem that severe, based on X-Rays. However, he remains comatose."

"Have you done an MRI or CT Scan?"

"We don't have that equipment here. He would need to be transferred to Cheyenne for those tests. At first, his condition did not allow us to move him. However, now that he has been stable for several days, the doctor will probably order that procedure."

"How did he get here? Who brought him?" Dave Stone wanted to know.

"A local ambulance company – he was found unconscious in town."

"Who found him?"

"I don't know? You would need to check with the Sheriff's office. A report was made."

"I want to see my, (he stopped short of saying brother) the patient."

"Certainly, Dr. Addison. This way, please."

The room was dark. His was the only bed there. Mark stopped short, staring at the crumpled lifeless-looking form, not unlike the images in his dreams, except for the bandages and the fact that he was in a hospital bed not on a roadside. He sat down by the bedside. Looking at the small arm and hand of his brother exposed above the covers. Tears came to his eyes as he said to the others, "Leave us alone, please."

He picked up the hand, kissing it gently. He stroked the long fingers and spoke softly, "It's me Timmy. It's Mark. Everything's going to be all right now. I'm going to take you home."

Mark was startled by an unmistakable squeezing of his hand. He knew this was his brother and he knew he had heard his voice. He sat there for a very long time just stroking the hand and telling him about all the things that were going on in Richmond.

"Michelle has a new boyfriend. His hair's longer than yours. And, I swear, he has more piercings than anyone I've ever seen."

"I wouldn't read too much into the hand squeezing, Dr. Addison," the resident surgeon had cautioned. "It could just be involuntary muscle contractions."

"I realize it could be, Doctor. But I don't think so."

"At any rate, I have to change his bandages today, so that will give you an opportunity to look at his face. That could help you make a more positive identification."

"Thank you. But, I'm certain this is Tim."

The bandages were removed later that afternoon and Mark was shocked by the injury and swelling but it was unmistakably the face of his brother Tim.

"I would like my brother moved to a larger hospital," he informed Dave Stone.

"You name the place and it will be done."

TEN

The chartered hospital jet left the runway of the small county airport and streaked eastward into the Wyoming sky, and, less than three hours later, landed at Richmond's Byrd International Airport, where a helicopter was waiting for the short transport to the Medical College of Virginia Hospital.

A team of surgeons and specialists were assembled to review the file from Wyoming and to analyze the results of the tests that were coming in. Mark had talked with Mary O'Riley several times from Wyoming and had phoned her after he arrived back in Richmond with his brother. She was truly relieved that the case of Timothy Addison seemed to be resolving with a less than catastrophic ending.

Patty was waiting at the hospital when the helicopter arrived. She greeted her husband with a kiss and warm embrace. She was happy that he and Tim were both safe and back in Richmond.

The head neurosurgeon, Dr. West approached Mark and Patty in the lounge.

"Dr. Addison, I am Dr. Gray West. We have the results of the CT Scan done on your brother. There are several small bone fragments which are pressing on and may have slightly penetrated the brain. We are preparing to operate, now. Everything else seems fine. I do not feel the injury to the brain is severe enough to prevent a full recovery."

"Thank you Dr. West. Please keep us posted. We will be right here."

Mark turned to his wife. "Have you spoken to Eric or Marianne?"

"Not in the past couple of days. They're out of town, in New York."

"Can you believe that pair? We're in the middle of a family crisis and they go to New York for some 'emergency' shopping."

"Now, be nice. We all deal with crisis and stress in our own way. Theirs seems to be by shopping," she said with a mischievous grin at her husband as she squeezed his arm.

"Have I told you I'm glad you're back?"

"Yes. I do believe you mentioned something about that. How are the girls, by the way?"

"They're fine. They have been extremely cooperative and solicitous of me during this whole thing. It's actually rather surprising."

"They're good girls, Michelle's Lenny not withstanding."

"Lenny isn't around, anymore. He was last week's news. This week it's Darren."

"And does Darren sport as many epidermal perforations as Lenny?"

"Not nearly as many."

"That's a relief."

"Darren is in to tattoos."

"No. Tell me it isn't so."

"I'm afraid it is."

"Aren't there any normal boys at that school?"

"I suspect the ones she is bringing home are the more normal ones."

"That is truly scary."

"I'm glad, in a way, we don't have boys."

"Me too, except, I don't like the idea of these types touching my daughters."

"I'm sure Pam and Michelle will respect your wishes."

"Yeah. Right after I'm elected King of the World."

Patty laughed in her girlish giggle, which Mark loved, squeezed his arm close again. It felt really good to have him back.

PART FOUR

Trooper Ed Pearson of the Colorado State Patrol was entering Interstate 70 heading west toward the Eisenhower Tunnel when he observed a green and gray Ford Bronco traveling the same direction, at a high rate of speed.

He immediately gave pursuit and contacted dispatch, "...in pursuit of a green and gray Ford Bronco, heading west on I-70. Request backup."

The driver of the Bronco showed no signs of stopping even though a total of three troopers were now in pursuit of his vehicle. The decision was made to set up a road block east of the tunnel.

As the Bronco rounded the last curve, approaching the road block at full speed, the driver hit the brakes hard and swerved just prior to crashing into the cruisers blocking his path. The vehicle flipped when it hit the shoulder of the road, becoming airborne for a short time then flipped twice more, before coming to rest on its side down the embankment.

Trooper Pearson called for crash support and medical personnel to the scene. "We have two unidentified males, in unknown condition here. But, it looks serious," he added.

A computer check of the Virginia license plate confirmed that the vehicle was stolen and the occupants were wanted for questioning in connection with, in addition to the vehicle theft, abduction, attempted murder and robbery.

Pearson approached the crash scene as the rescue and paramedic teams arrived and started working, trying to free the two men from the vehicle. Both it was determined were alive though injured and losing a lot of blood. He informed the person in charge that the men were wanted by the Federal Marshal and they were riding a stolen vehicle.

"Why does that not surprise me," was the response.

When the two men were removed from the vehicle, identification showed them to be Billy Whaley, aged thirty-seven, of Ft. Collins who, apparently not belted in, had been partially ejected through the windshield, and Marvin Baldwin, the driver aged forty of Taos, NM. They also found two guns and alcohol in the vehicle. A medivac chopper had arrived to transport the two back to Denver for treatment.

"There's a waste of taxpayer dollars," one trooper opined in a rather cynical tone.

"That's life," Pearson said with a shrug.

TWO

The dimly lit hospital room was quiet; there were two beds, but only one was occupied; the blinds on the window were drawn against the late evening sun sinking over the city's west end.

The woman had been sitting by the bed for more than an hour, even though the patient had not moved. Bandages covering his entire head, obscured everything except the eyes, nose and mouth. Tubes supplied fluids, oxygen, and carried away bodily waste, while wires attached to various locations monitored bodily functions – heart rate, temperature, and blood pressure.

She sat there in the dark hoping, praying that this young man, someone she really did not even know, who had become such a central part of her life – almost an obsession over the past several weeks would soon open those haunting eyes from the picture. That he would rejoin the conscious world of the living. She also prayed that God would somehow intervene and correct this injustice and that the animals, who had inflicted these grave injuries, causing such suffering would be rendered the appropriate punishment, both in this world and in the one to come.

Stroking the fine-boned hand, she told him about her day. She related seeing what could be the final flock of birds in migratory formations heading south. Obviously they were looking for warmer areas to wait out the coming winter months of the north. She recalled how the chilling November wind had grabbed at her coat as she was crossing Broad Street on her way to the hospital.

She told him of the bands of homeless people jockeying for warmer sleeping locations around the downtown areas of Grace and Main Street. Finally, leaving the room, sadly and reluctantly, she wiped a tear from her eye as she had each evening for the past two weeks since he had undergone neuro-surgery to remove bone fragments from his brain. The doctors said that medically he was fine; that the injuries needed time to heal; that he could wake from his coma at anytime. However, they also cautioned that the longer he remained in this state, the slimmer his chance of recovery.

She scheduled her visits for a time which coincided with the break in the family visitation. She wasn't exactly avoiding them, she just didn't want to see them or be seen by them. She had her own private and personal reasons for coming. Emerging into the now dark cold of the evening, she doubted anew her wisdom in leaving her car at work five blocks away, as she pulled her coat tightly around her waist, turned her collar up against the wind and headed back into the night. She noted Broad Street had only moderate traffic since the evening rush hour had ended. She walked quickly and soon arrived safely back at the municipal parking garage. Her mind was filled with thoughts of the injured young man as she entered the Downtown Expressway and headed west toward her apartment-home. She was certain that he had squeezed her hand today when she was telling him about the migration of the birds and again when she laughingly related the story of her little nieces' birthday party over the weekend, with all the chocolate cake you could hold – and how it was the best cake ever, her grandmother's secret recipe.

This was all quite insane, she told herself. Why was she obsessing over one of countless numbers of people whose names and files crossed her desk during any given year?

Why had this one affected her so? Why had he haunted her since the first day she saw his picture? Why had her professional involvement become so personal? Why did she personally want to go to Colorado and spit on the perpetrators of this crime against another human? This wasn't like her at all.

THREE

Arriving at her darkened apartment, barren of personal touches, so that it more closely resembled transient housing than someone's personal home, she turned on the lights, one by one, till all the rooms were well lit – she had endured enough dark for one day – hoping the light would improve her mood.

Looking around at the rooms, she was shocked to realize, as if for the first time, even though she had lived here for more than a year now, there was nothing of her personally here. She had planned to decorate, but she just hadn't come up with the right scheme. Her mother had offered help, but she knew she wasn't up for that. Somehow, the picture of a white canopy bed in her bedroom with frilly curtains on the windows always came to mind when her mother suggested how much fun it would be to do her place together. Oh, well, she meant well, at least.

As she walked by the hall table, the red blinking light of the answering machine demanded attention. She pressed the "new-message" button, on her way to the kitchen for a drink. The machine beeped, then announced, "You have three new messages…"

Message one: "Hi. It's Ben. I tried to catch you after work today, but I guess you left in a hurry. Call me!"

Message two: "Hello, Dear. It's your mother. Just checking to see if you're okay since we haven't heard from you in a while. Your father sends his love."

Message three: "It's me again. I just remembered we are supposed to take the girls to the circus this weekend. Since I haven't seen you, I wanted to let you know if you're busy or something, it's okay. Mary? What's going on? Call me."

"End of messages…" Beep.

She was sitting in a chair, still wearing her coat when the last message finished. She replayed the words in her mind, "…Mary? What's going on?" What indeed was going on – an injured man in a hospital room was robbing her of her sanity – that's what was going on. She had to get over this. She had to do something.

A tear slid down the side of her cheek as she forced herself up out of the chair, wondering why moving her body seemed like such a Herculean task, she headed for the door and the night beyond, from which she had just emerged.

Being at home wasn't the answer tonight. She drove to Lakeside, hoping that the usually present smells of food and people at her parents house would help her climb out of this hole she had fallen into. As she made the turn onto the street which had been home to her family for over thirty years, seeing her father's car in the drive and all the lights in the house blazing, a small smile came to her face – all hope was not lost.

"Mary. What a wonderful surprise," her mother gushed with enthusiasm as she opened the door. "Come in. Take your coat off. Have you eaten? There's food in the kitchen. Your father and I just finished. We would have waited if we had known. Are you okay Dear? You seem so quiet."

Her mother was the only person she had ever known who could give you a stream of conscious thought without let-up for an answer.

"I'm fine, Mom. I just felt a little lonely tonight and I thought some company and some good home cooking might improve my mood."

"Well. I'm certainly glad you did. We've got all this food left over and I was just getting ready to decide what to do with it."

"Mom. It looks like you cooked for a family of twelve. Don't you know how to cook for two?"

"Well. You never know when someone may drop by and the leftovers come in handy if you don't feel like cooking the next day."

"And just when have you ever served leftovers for dinner?" she asked this question as she was taking a place at the table, having heaped a pile of food – meat loaf, potatoes, bread and beans – on the plate she had taken.

"I do. Occasionally," her mother said, sounding rather defensive.

"Where's dad?"

"He's in the basement. Working on his latest project. You know your father."

"Is he all right? How's the cholesterol?"

"He's fine. The doctor says his cholesterol level is normal.

He's been taking garlic and it seemed to work."

"What's he building, now? Another bird feeder?"

"I'm not sure. He said something about a magazine rack and telephone stand."

"Your house is full of his little projects. He's going to have to add another room."

"You know how your father enjoys his hobbies. I don't really mind. It keeps him busy. He could be sleeping in front of the TV, after all."

"Hey, I have a great idea. I think it's time to decorate my apartment and I could use some book shelves to get all my books off the floor and out of boxes. Do you suppose Dad would be willing?"

"I'm sure he would be glad to. Do you want me to ask him? Do you need my help?" she asked rather hopefully.

Almost blinded by the vision of the canopy bed and frilly curtains coming into her mind again, she started to say, "No, thanks." However, looking at her mother's downcast eyes and all the food on the table, realizing her mother also needed some little projects, she stopped the fork-full of food half way to her mouth and said, "Sure, Mom. I would love to have your help." Rewarded instantly by her mother's smile, she saw the wheels turning – her mom was already mentally buying yards of fabric and sewing curtains.

"But," she added cautiously. "No frills. Okay, Mom?"

"Whatever you say Dear."

Oh, God, she thought. She had really done it. There would be no stopping her mother now. She would end up living in an apartment with embroidered sofa pillows and ruffled curtains.

"By the way," her mother said changing her tone. "I almost forgot. Ben called here looking for you. He sounded worried. Is everything all right – with you and Ben, I mean?"

"Ben called here? Why? He left a message on my machine. It didn't sound that urgent to me."

"Ben's such a nice man…" Her voice trailed off at the look on her daughter's face.

"Mom. Don't start about Ben and me. I'm not going to marry Ben and there is nothing to discuss. Besides, I'm not so sure about things anymore."

"Things? What things? Ben loves you very much."

"Ben thinks he loves me, Mom. But, I'm not even sure he knows who I am. Sometimes I don't even know. Sometimes it feels like I'm a missing person."

"That sounds awfully ominous and mysterious."

Her mother had been in the daily vocabulary improvement book again, she could tell. She had never heard her mother use ominous in conversation before.

"There's nothing ominous or mysterious about it, Mom. I'm just facing some rather tough decisions. That's all."

"Work related, or personal?"

"Both, I'm afraid."

"Maybe you should take some time off. You haven't really had a vacation since you went to Myrtle Beach three years ago."

"I think I could use some time off. But, I can't. Not right now, anyway."

"Now that really does sound ominous."

She reached over patted her mother's hand and smiled. "Don't worry. Everything's fine. By the way, how are Beth and Tracy?"

"They're both fine. Beth took Angela to the Pediatrician for a checkup today. Everything is just great. She's a normal healthy four-year old."

"I could have told her that after spending last weekend with them, and I wouldn't have charged her a hundred bucks for an office call. That child has more energy than any I've ever seen. She makes Megan look like a she's the one that needs a checkup."

"Oh, now, Megan is just a quiet little girl. She never was energetic the way Angela is."

"For which I am certain my sister is thankful."

"Yes, I rather imagine so. Although, having a quiet-reserved child can be just as difficult as raising one that is the opposite. You have to try much harder with Megan to get her interested and find out what she wants and what she is thinking."

"Well, all I can say is, may I never be blessed with becoming a mother."

"What a horrible thing to wish for." Her mother said with a genuine look of shock on her face.

"Why? I don't think everyone is necessarily cut out to be a parent. And, I think I'm rather fortunate to realize that I am one of those who isn't. I don't think I could cope with having a child, like either of my nieces."

"Well, I personally think you would make a fine mother. You have qualities that neither of your sisters have. You just have to want to be a parent – it's not that difficult."

"Mom. In my job I have seen far too much evidence of what can happen when children are born to people that never should have been parents. No thank you!"

"But, you would be a good mother. You wouldn't be cruel – that's not you. I know it."

"The absence of cruelty does not necessarily equal a loving family relationship, Mother. I have seen teenage runaways from families where there was never a hint of physical cruelty. You have to be loving and supportive of your children – positive actions are required; not just a lack of negative actions and feelings."

"Well, I still say..."

"Mom," she interrupted. "New subject. Please!"

Both women were quiet for some time after that and grateful for her father's emerging from his basement workshop.

"Thought I heard voices up here," he said walking over to his daughter for a hug.

"Why didn't you come and fetch me, Sue?"

"Oh, well, Mary's been eating and we were talking women-talk. You wouldn't have been interested. But, our daughter has finally decided to decorate her apartment and she wants our help. Can you believe it?"

He certainly could not. Looking at his eldest daughter, knowing her feelings about her mother's tastes in decorating, searching for a clue as to what must have transpired, prior to his arrival.

"Have you lost your mind, or something?"

"Bill. What an awful thing to say."

"I'm sorry, honey. But, the picture of Mary living in a house full of pastel ruffled things is just a bit too much. Come on. You're kidding me, aren't you?"

"Well, William O'Riley. I'll have you know that I am perfectly capable of working with the fabrics and colors of Mary's choice. Just because I prefer one style does not mean a thing. She asked me to help and I said I would."

"Okay. Don't get your feathers all ruffled at me."

"Besides. She wants you to help, too. She needs bookshelves."

"Bookshelves?" He got a starry-eyed look. "You want bookshelves? I can give you all the bookshelves you want."

Doubting the wisdom anew of her suggestions, Mary now saw her apartment filled with wall-to-wall bookshelves in every room.

"Nothing fancy, Dad," she cautioned. "Just a couple of plain bookcases; something that I could take with me when I move."

"Oh, sure," he said, feeling only slightly daunted. "I can do plain, too. Plain's good – if that's what you want."

"Well," Mary said looking at her watch. "I've got to go. It's almost your bedtime."

"Nonsense, why it's early," her mother protested. "We haven't even looked at any decorating books yet."

"I know, but I'm kind of tired," she replied – realizing that she was. "We can start on that this weekend."

"Well. All right. Thanks for dropping by."

"Bye Mom. Dad," she said giving them both a hug as she was leaving. "I'll call you about this weekend."

"Bye, Dear. Give our love to Ben," her mother called through the screen where she would stand, as usual, watching her daughter till she was safely in her car, having locked the doors, belted herself in, and had driven away.

FOUR

Mary sat in her office all morning, pretending to be absorbed in one file or another. At eleven-thirty, Ben Stewart opened her door and walked in.

"Hey. Remember me? My name's Ben."

She looked up, giving him a smile, "Hi. I'm sorry. I've been awfully busy lately. I'm really not avoiding you."

"Funny. It sure feels that way."

"Sorry."

For a moment he thought she was actually going to start flipping pages in the file, again. He started to leave, but then decided to try again.

"Mary. What's going on?"

"What do you mean?"

"You know what I mean. We haven't been on a date in over two weeks. Is there someone else?"

"No. Of course not."

"Why do I not believe you? Mary, at least be honest with me. If there is someone else – someone you've fallen in love with, please tell me. You don't have to avoid me and hope I'll go away. Just say the words and I will."

"Ben. I don't know what's going on right now. There isn't really anyone else – I mean, I'm not going out with anyone else. I think I just need some time."

"All right, Mary. If you need some time, that's fine. But, for God's sake, please don't ask me to wait forever. I don't think I can do that. I won't do that."

"Ben. You and your girls have been three of the most important people in my life for a very long time. You will always be important to me. But, I don't know that I will ever be able to marry you – be a wife to you and a mother to them – and that isn't fair, to any of us. I should feel differently about this. I should be eager to have a family – to be a part of your family."

"But you're not. Is that it?"

"I'm afraid so."

"Fine, Mary. You do your thinking and I guess I will do some thinking of my own. Then just maybe if we're thinking the same thing, we can get together. If not, I guess that life. Huh?"

His voice seemed to be trembling, which was inconsistent with the look of fire in his eyes. Mary had never seen Ben Stewart so angry and upset. To be the focus and cause of his ire was quite unsettling to her. She looked down at her files, blinking back the tears clouding her eyes, as he strode out of her office, slamming her door behind him, silencing the roar of the outer office as he went. She knew her face was beet-red and that everyone was staring at her through her glass partitioned wall.

After staring at the same page of the same file for several minutes, trying to regain her composure, she heard her door open again. Looking up, she fully expected to see Ben returning with an "I didn't mean it," look.

"Mary," her boss Jim Dillon spoke as he walked in. "I want to talk with you about a couple of new files that just came in."

"Jim," she said without looking up. "I think I need to take some time off."

"What? You? Are you all right?"

"No. I'm not all right," she said with tears in her eyes.

"What's wrong? Was that a fight just now with Ben? You two not getting along?"

"I don't know what's going on, Jim. I just think I need to take some time."

"Fine, Mary. You have plenty of personal and vacation time. Take whatever you need. When do you want to start?"

"Right now, I'm afraid."

"Okay. I'll have Larry Davis come in. You can bring him up to speed on your files."

"I'm sorry, Jim. I can't do that. I mean I really need to leave right now. All my files are documented – he can pickup where I left off. I'm sorry," she repeated.

"No problem, Mary."

Jim Dillon was deeply troubled by this side of Mary O'Riley. A side he had never seen before. She was always in control of her emotions and any situation. Some rather unkind gossip about her had made its way round the office.

They called her, "Ice water Mary."

"Thanks, Jim," she said as she stood taking her coat from the rack by the door,

"I'll call you."

"No problem," he repeated.

As she was walking away, she heard him calling, "Larry. You want to come in here please."

Riding the elevator down to the lobby, she felt a sudden relief, as if a weight had been lifted off her shoulders. It was then she realized she would never go back. And, she realized something else, it felt great!"

FIVE

Mary crossed Broad Street heading for MCV Hospital. It was midday, unlike her usual evening visiting over the past months. She wasn't sure who would be there, but she didn't care. All she knew was that she had to go.

She rode the elevator up, unbuttoning her heavy coat as she walked down the corridor to the west wing and the room she had visited daily for the past two and a half weeks. Relieved that no one was there, she went in and took her seat by the bed.

She looked at the face. The bandages were mostly gone – the visible injuries healed. But still he was missing.

Sitting there in the dimly lit room, feeling a flood of emotion rising inside, she squeezed the hand of the man who had unknowingly caused her to look at so many aspects of her life as if for the very first time.

Startled when she felt a very strong squeeze in return, she looked up, saw the opened brown eyes looking at her. He smiled, squeezing her hand again, holding on when she loosened her grip, as the well of tears she had been holding back released.

"Oh my God," she said with a rush of emotion. Fighting back the wash of impending tears, she managed enough composure to say, "You're back."

"Have I been gone? And, if so, where exactly have I come back to?" he asked, the smile never fading the grasp on her hand not lessened.

"I'd say, yes. You have been gone, for quite sometime, but you're back safe and sound in good old Richmond, Virginia."

"That's funny," he said. "Last thing I remember I was in New Mexico, fishing. How exactly did I get back to Richmond?"

"You came back first class in a Government Issue hospital jet."

"Wow. That makes me feel important. I'm Tim, by the way. But I guess you already know that. You seem so familiar to me. But, I don't think I know you. And yet, I feel like I know you intimately. Can you help me out here?"

"I'm sorry. I'm Mary. And, let's just say, we've spent a lot of time together lately."

She kept looking into those eyes which had seemed so sad, so disturbing in the photo, yet they really weren't at all – they were soulful, and from all appearance had the ability to look into a person's very being, discerning fact from fiction; right from wrong; sincere from insincere.

"Okay, Mary. This must have been quality time we spent. 'Cause, I feel like I know a lot about you."

Suddenly, it seemed to have just occurred to her that he was out of his coma. That she needed to tell someone.

"I need to tell someone you're awake. I'll get a nurse or a doctor. I'll call your brother."

"Don't go," Tim said holding her hand tightly. "They'll find out soon enough. For now it's just our secret. Mary," he said her name with adoration, almost reverently.

"Okay, Tim."

"How long have I been here?"

"About six weeks. What's the last thing you remember?"

"I'm not sure. I think I remember the cause of this headache and then the lights went out – but I don't want to talk about that. I want to know about you. Who are you? What stroke of good fortune brought you into my life?"

"I'm afraid it was the same occurrence, or at least the events leading up to it, though I'm not sure I would call it good fortune, that put the lights out."

"I don't understand?"

"Well. I'm Mary O'Riley, I was working in the Missing Persons Unit at Police Headquarters when your picture was tossed on my desk, courtesy of your brothers."

"You mean," he said sounding rather disappointed. "This is all in the line of duty to you? Does your job include a bedside vigil for each case?"

She felt his grip almost loosen on her hand.

"I'm afraid not," she replied holding his hand in both hers. The smile returned to his face and his grip tightened. "You see," she paused, "This will probably sound crazy, I haven't been able to get you out of my mind since I first saw your picture. So when they brought you back here, I came by, just to see how you were, I told myself, and I haven't been able to stop coming back. I've been here every night, talking to you telling you about my days, my family and holding your hand."

"Well, then I guess I should thank you."

"You already have. You opened those eyes. Has anyone ever told you that you have remarkable eyes, by the way?"

"Not that I can recall," he said showing signs of getting tired.

"I've tired you out during your first moments of consciousness in weeks. I'll get the nurse."

"No. Don't go. I don't want you to ever leave me." He said seriously – insistently.

"Okay," she said, rather uncertainly. "I'm right here. But, we should really let the nurse know before you go to sleep."

She reached over and pressed the Nurse Call button. Within seconds, it seemed, the nurse appeared in the doorway.

"Who rang that call button? Is Mr. Addison awake?" She demanded as she made her way over to the bedside.

Mary answered, "I pressed the button, and yes, Mr. Addison is awake."

The nurse was leaning over Tim's bed, shining a light in his eyes, talking in an exaggerated loud voice. "Can you hear me? Can you see my fingers? Do you know where you are?"

"Would you please stop yelling at me?" Tim responded. "I have a splitting headache."

Leaving the room with only a "Humph," they soon heard the same nurse's voice over the paging system. "Dr. Marshall. Dr. Paul Marshall. Please call…" The page was repeated several times in the next few minutes.

Tim's eyes closed, but the smile never left his face as he held on tightly, afraid to loosen his grip, afraid he would lose his hold on consciousness and reality, if indeed this was reality and not a dream.

For Mary, thoughts, mostly questions without answers began racing through her mind. She had really never considered what to do when Tim awoke. She had certainly not expected him to continue holding on to her as she had been holding on to him in the past few weeks. This really complicated things and she hadn't a clue as to how to straighten them out – or even if she really needed to try to straighten anything out. This could be a case of fixation, not unlike that of a newly hatched chick bonding with the first live creature he sees.

Mary heard voices and the sound of fast paced footfalls approaching the room.

"How long has he been awake?" The doctor asked as he entered the room, though he didn't seem to be directing the question to her, nor even aware she was in the room.

"Less than thirty minutes, I'd guess," the nurse responded.

Shining another light into each of his eyes, as he held up the eyelid, without looking in her direction, he asked, "Are you the wife? Girlfriend?"

It took Mary a moment to react. "No. Just a friend," she said softly, noting the squeeze of her hand, overlapping the doctor's continued line of rapid questioning.

"Take my hand please."

Tim's reply, "I don't even know you," which caused Mary to stifle a giggle was not appreciated by the solemn-faced doctor.

"Squeeze my hand please. Excellent." The doctor looked at Mary for the first time and gave her a half-smile. "You may want to wait outside."

"She's attached," Tim answered holding up his other hand.

"Very well," the doctor said with a shrug as he continued his examination of Tim Addison uncovering and unbuttoning as he went till he had checked for reflexes, reactions and responses to the bottoms of Tim's feet.

"This is really most excellent," Doctor Marshall commented in summation. "There does not appear to be any injury to the nervous system. Has Mark Addison been Notified?" he asked in the general direction of the nurse it seemed, though Mary wasn't really sure.

"Yes Doctor. I called his office right after I paged you. He should be here shortly."

Mary felt a twinge of concern, almost panic at the prospect of facing Mark Addison, whom she had been unable to inform of her visitation. She knew holding on to his brother's hand was going to take some explaining and she wasn't sure she had a ready explanation.

The doctor and nurse left the room together, "Call me when Mark gets here…"

"Yes Doctor."

SIX

They were alone again, his eyes were closed, though he was awake she could tell.

Turning his head toward her he asked, "Will you marry me?"

Startled by the question, she searched his eyes for a hint of a joke. Finding none, she became really confused and flustered. "You don't even know me, Tim."

"Yes I do. I know you better than anyone I've met in my entire life."

"How can you be so certain of that? For all you know, I could have a husband and family."

"I'll wait till you get rid of him, since you're obviously no longer in love. As for the kids, I love kids, you can keep them."

Looking into those eyes, she knew she was hopelessly lost in this crazy situation.

"I think that bump on the head has damaged your mental powers. You're insane."

"Maybe. But, if I am, I don't ever want to be sane again. I've been there and this is better. "

Mark Addison had entered the room, unheard. More than a little confused by what he had just heard and what he was seeing, he forced a smile at Mary O'Riley as he grasped his brother's free hand.

"Timmy, my boy. I can't tell you how happy I am to see you awake and in such, apparently, good spirits. Doctor Marshall says you're fine. We may get to take you home soon."

"Hello, Mark. How are you?"

"I'm fine, now. I tell you, though, I've been more than a little worried. But you have apparently been in very good hands," he said flashing Mary a questioning look.

"You two know each other, don't you," Tim asked.

"Yes." Mary responded.

"And how are you Sgt. O'Riley?" Mark asked rather sternly.

"I am well, Dr. Addison," Mary responded in kind.

"Tim, you should get some rest now," Mark spoke up. "I need to talk with Sgt. O'Riley about Denver."

"She's never leaving my side. You can talk here."

Tempted by the offer of a temporary shield from the barrage of questions that must have been in Mark Addison's head and the near rage in his eyes, she realized it had to be done.

"I'm sorry, Tim. I really have to go. I'll be back later."

"Promise?"

"Promise."

He squeezed her hand once more before letting go, the pain flickering across his face was almost too much for her. She got up and followed Mark out of the room, her head lowered in expectation of what was to come. The doctor did not say a word or slow his pace till he reached a waiting area down the hall.

He stared at the woman, for what seemed an eternity, not sure his anger was justified, feeling totally confused, if not betrayed.

Unable to endure his look or the silence any longer, Mary started to speak, but was only able to say, "Mark," before he raised his hand cutting her off.

"So you are the mysterious female visitor the nurses reported?"

He paused looking at her as if waiting for a response, though they both knew he wasn't finished.

"I don't know what's going on here; what your game is; but I don't like the picture I'm getting. Are you some kind of sick person who's become obsessed with an incapacitated man you've never met? I know this happens frequently in hospitals and in homes where comatose patients are kept, I just never expected it to happen to my brother. I don't really want to know what you did or thought of doing, I just want to know why my brother? Why my family? I trusted you with my deepest concerns. I thought you and I had become friends. And now, this. I don't even know you."

"Mark, please. I know this looks very bad. And believe me, there is nothing you could say to me that I haven't already said to myself."

"Oh, I doubt that."

"I'm sorry if I have hurt you in any way. That was not my intent, I assure you."

"Well sorry doesn't help this situation. I intend to report you to your superior officer. I will have you fired for this."

"I'm afraid you're a little late. I've already quit my job. Unofficially, anyway."

Mark Addison had been pacing back and forth in the small room like a caged animal seeking release from his prison confinement, knowing there was no way out, yet never giving up hope that the bars would one day part providing escape. Then without a word, he stopped pacing and sat down in the chair beside her peering into her eyes, hoping for some answer for some reason to prevail.

"Mary," he said in a tone so quiet it stunned her like an electrical shock. "I don't want to come off here like some raving lunatic," he continued softly. "Help me out, please. Am I attacking you because I am unable to adequately show the emotions I feel at my brother's recovery? Are you an innocent bystander, Mary? Am I crazy?"

She looked at the older brother, the man who had been consumed with guilt and worry by his brother's disappearance and injuries over the past two months. She felt an urge to reach out to him and make his pain go away – the same as she had felt on countless other occasions when some other person's loved one had been lost.

"Mark, you are not crazy. Trust me. I have seen crazy reactions since I first came to work in the Department. Yours doesn't even approach crazy. I know what I did was highly unprofessional, inexplicable, yet I will try to explain. When I first came here to see your brother, I was looking for some sort of closure to this case. I wanted to see for myself that Tim was safe, if not yet sound. I can't describe to you the rush of emotions I felt when I looked at him for the first time – lifeless, yet there was life and even vigor there, trying to get out. I have seen many people in similar situations, hooked up to machines; their bodily functions continue, but they are already dead. There is nothing or no one there. But, Tim wasn't like that. He looked alive. His muscles were flexed and ready for action. There was almost a magnetism that drew me to him. I touched his hand lightly and the fingers curled – I swear they did. Then I left.

I returned the following day, then the next, then the next. I began sitting by his bedside, holding his hand in mine, telling him what the weather outside was like. What my day had been like. About a birthday party I attended for my nieces. About my family. All this began and continued, and I assure you that nothing else ever even entered my mind, until today when he awoke. I cannot express the happiness and joy of relief I felt when those eyes opened, looking into mine for the first time. As I said, I am sorry if my actions have hurt you or anyone else. I should have told you I was visiting him, but I couldn't really find the right words or the time. Visiting your brother and talking – just talking to him has been therapeutic for me as well. My life has been so strange during the past several years, almost as if I had become one of my missing persons' cases. I wasn't there, just like the countless others I spent my time looking for, instead of trying to find myself. I went through the motions of living, but I wasn't alive. Being around Tim makes me feel alive, partly I think, because he was and is so alive, so vital. I don't want to lose that feeling. Please don't ask me to give him up. I don't think I can."

Having sat unmoving during her entire speech, Mark was now at a loss. He didn't know what to think, what to feel. Quite possibly, the actions of the woman, for whom he had felt such anger, had single handedly pulled his brother out of his coma. Medical literature emphasized the necessity of what she had done. Stimulating the brain by touch and talking are paramount in the recovery regimen of people suffering strokes and brain trauma. He felt ashamed that this woman, whom he had assailed for her attention to his brother, had given the therapy that he and the rest of his family had been too busy to provide.

"I guess I really should thank you," he began, choking back emotion. "Your visitation and actions probably helped him to finally snap out of the coma. I apologize for my accusations and insinuations. I know you never meant anyone any harm."

"Thank you. I guess I should go now."

"I'm sure. Though I really do need to talk to you about Denver. I got a call from there today."

"What's up in Denver?"

"One of our suspects has died as the result of injuries in a car crash following a police chase."

"Which one?"

"Whaley. The one who used the credit card. The U.S. Attorney's office is afraid they don't have much of a case against the other man, who claims he was just along for the ride."

"Are they going to trial?"

"Probably not. Unless Tim recovers enough to recall the events and will testify."

"I asked him what he remembers, but I think it's hazy to him."

"The details may come back."

"Let's hope. I'd hate to see this creep get off."

"You and me both."

SEVEN

New snow was falling on top of the white blanket already on the ground, as the Delta Jetliner descended from the eastern sky for its landing at Denver International Airport that March afternoon.

She looked at her traveling companion who was staring out the window in childlike amazement as the ground rushed up to meet them. "Nervous?" she asked.

"A little, I guess."

"It's all right. I'm here."

They had said little during the entire flight, now they made small talk about the weather, and the throng of nameless faces in the crowd, when one of the faces approached them.

"Mr. Addison? Ms. O'Riley?"

"Yes," they replied almost in unison.

"I'm Stephen Archer from the U.S. Attorney's office. I hope you folks had a nice flight. Did you come in direct from Richmond?"

"No. We flew through Dulles."

"If you will come with me, we have a car waiting to take you to your hotel. I'll try to brief you on the way. The trial of Mr. Baldwin started last week. The prosecutor, wanting to have some element of surprise, only announced to the court yesterday that Mr. Addison would be making a guest appearance. You should have seen the look on the faces of Baldwin and his attorney. Of course, the attorney objected and asked for a delay to prepare for, I believe it was, '…the unexpected grievous and prejudicial impact this appearance would have on his client's defense…"

"What does all that mean," Tim asked as they made their way down the long concourse, the crowd seeming to part like the waters of the Biblical Red Sea, for the party.

"It means," Agent Archer responded, "you can tell the jury the S.O.B. is lying about just being along for the ride, which he claims. He says he never laid eyes on you."

"And what happens if I can't?" Tim wondered aloud, not sure his clouded memory and tortured dreams of the events would be of any particular advantage to anyone other than this Baldwin guy.

"I don't want to steal the prosecutor's thunder. But, a lineup at the county jail has been prearranged and since Mr. Baldwin is an inmate at the jail, he will be in the lineup. In preparation for this, and so he doesn't think anything of it, he has been in several lineups during the recent weeks. If you pick this guy out of the line, Bingo!"

"And if not?" Mary wanted to know.

Archer shrugged.

As they made their way out of the terminal, Mary noticed that Tim was beginning to shiver, either from the welcoming bone-chilling Rocky Mountain Spring air, or from the fact of being back in Colorado, something he had not been exactly eagerly anticipating.

"Cold?" she asked him.

"Not exactly. I'm all right," he said raising himself, refusing assistance, from the wheel chair he had reluctantly agreed to accept, for the half-mile trek to the outside world.

The stifling heat inside the van, which they found less tolerable than the cold, prompted a request for air as they motored away from the airport and toward the hotel near the Federal Courthouse in downtown Denver.

Tim Addison was still shivering when they arrived at the Marriott, causing Mary to worry about him anew. When they reached their suite, she ordered hot soup and hot tea from room service. "Please hurry," she urged.

"I'm going to run you a hot bath. I'm really worried about that chill you've got."

"It's fine. I'll be all right," he said fighting to keep his teeth from chattering.

Checking the time, she picked up the phone again. "Yes. Could you ring Dr. Mark Addison, please? Thank you."

After a long pause, the operator came back on and informed her there was no answer, offering to page him in the hotel common areas.

"Please do. Ask him to call his brother's room. Thank you."

She ran the hottest bath imaginable, ignoring the complaints and objections of Tim.

"Don't be such a baby," she teased. "I'm going to leave now and don't you dare run cold water in there. This is for your own good."

"Won't you stay and scrub my back," he asked, seeming momentarily recovered from his chilling.

"Big phony," she said throwing a wash cloth at him as she left the room.

The hot soup, fresh bread and hot tea arrived just as she left the bathroom, shaking her head at the faked scalded-dog yelp he let out when his big toe tested the water. She realized she was very hungry when she smelled the aroma of the soup, finding it hard to refrain from digging in without Tim.

He emerged from the bathroom, pink and wrinkled like a newborn. "I told you that water was too hot," he whined.

"Baby. You'll survive. Have some food. Are you feeling better, by the way?"

"I think so. I'll be able to tell for sure when the feeling comes back to my body."

"Well, at least you're not cold anymore."

"That's for sure. I doubt I will ever be cold again. And if I am, I won't complain to you about it."

The telephone rang just as they finished the meal.

"Hello. Yes, Mark this is Mary. We just arrived about an hour ago. Sure, please do. You should probably take a look at Tim. He had quite a chill when we got here."

"Okay. We'll see you in a few minutes."

Mark Addison arrived in about ten minutes, complete with the official-looking doctor's black bag, exchanging friendly greetings with both.

"So how's the trial going?" Mary broached the topic they were seeming to avoid.

"I'm not sure, really. The prosecution doesn't have much to offer. Donna Isom testified that Billy Whaley, who was in the stolen vehicle that Baldwin was driving, had attempted to use Tim's credit card, upon which she called the police."

"How did she know he wasn't Tim?"

"Seems that Whaley came from her hometown. I gather there was some sort of story she really didn't want to go into. Of course, the defense attorney protested asking that her entire testimony be stricken, which the judge is taking under advisement. The defense attorney's only cross examination was, '…have you ever seen Mr. Baldwin.' Her answer being 'No', he said thank you very much, no more questions."

"So basically their defense is going to be, blame it all on the dead guy."

"Basically. But, hopefully, little brother will be able to put an end to that," he said looking at Tim hopefully. Then asked with much concern, "Anything, yet?"

"Not unless you count bad dreams, complete with monsters."

EIGHT

The Denver County jail brought back a flood of memories to Mary O'Riley of all the visits she had made to similar facilities. They were all the same, she realized. This could be any of a thousand different lockups in a thousand different counties.

Tim seemed extremely nervous again, as they entered the line-up viewing room, realizing that the spotlight of attention was soon to be focused directly on him. He wasn't sure he wanted to put a face with the dark images that haunted his dreams and he was certain he didn't want to be here.

Sensing his reluctance and uneasiness, Mary took his hand squeezing it as she had so many times before. The familiar contact seemed to alleviate some of his discomfort as they sat down in front of the one-way mirrored viewing window. A parade of felons made their way across the elevated platform to their respective designated spots.

Tim's heart began racing, images of dread and terror filled his mind as he saw the moon-faced almost giant of a man, a visage he had prayed never to have to look at again, lumbering across the stage.

Feeling panic rising, unable to breathe, he was mentally transported and was once again bound and gagged on the back seat of his Bronco. The two men laughed and drank beer as they sped through the night, debating if they should dump his dead body in Colorado or across the border. The wicked sneer of the man standing in the Denver police line-up glared at him over the seat back.

Sweat was streaming down his face and neck when the agent from the U.S. Attorney's office asked him again, "Mr. Addison? Do you recognize anyone in the lineup?"

The voice sounded like it was coming through a filter of some sort which caused the words to be garbled and distorted. His eyes were fixed yet unfocused, his vision clouded by the perspiration running in his eyes.

He stared out the side window of the speeding vehicle, looking up at the millions of stars in the Colorado night. In dread and terror, he wondered if this would be his last night of viewing the heavenly bodies. He prayed silently, something he realized he had not done since he was a child, asking only for the courage to endure this ordeal – if he was to die, may it be with dignity, he beseeched the Almighty. He prayed again as he sat in the Denver lineup viewing room, for calm – of the same kind he remembered receiving that night, which seemed from another lifetime.

"Tim," his brother spoke. "Are you all right? Do you need something? Can we get you a drink of water?"

"No," he thought he said, though he could not be sure, through the sensation of choking caused by the filthy rag that had been stuffed in his mouth. "That's him," he finally whispered loud enough for all close by to hear.

"You sure?" the officer wanted to know. "Which man?"

"The big guy in the middle. I'll never forget that face and those eyes," he said knowing he would never again be able to rid himself of that image, of that sneering smile, of those words.

"What's wrong pretty boy? You need your momma?" He heard the near hysterical laughter of both men in the front of his vehicle.

"You got awfully pretty hair and skin," the voice continued in his mind as the nauseating feeling of being touched by the beefy sweaty hand and the skin-crawling result returned causing him to tremble.

The lineup concluded, they helped him out of his seat and back outside into the cold mountain air, his perspiration soaked clothing becoming like a body-wrap ice pack instantly. He started shivering again, feeling the need to vomit and weak from the experience.

Tim felt he was going to pass out from the ordeal. His head was reeling and pounding. Strange, he recalled, he had prayed for unconsciousness to overtake him and deliver him from the experiences of that surreal night which seemed a lifetime ago. Now, he was fighting off the loss of conscious thought and being. He wanted to make sure Baldwin would pay for what he was put through.

NINE

The Denver courtroom was hot and airless as they wheeled Tim Addison into the room for his appearance, following the announcement by the prosecutor, "Your honor, at this time, we call Timothy Addison to the stand."

The defense attorney sprang to his feet, shouting over the murmur of the court room, "Your Honor, I renew my objection to this witness. The prosecutor has deliberately withheld information about the appearance of this witness from the defense. Furthermore, they have made no connection between the victim and my client."

The judge banged his gavel demanding, "Order. Order in this courtroom."

However, his action did little to quiet the room. "Counselors, approach the bench."

"Mr. Hughes, do you have anything to offer?"

"Your Honor, Mr. Addison's name has always been on the list of potential witnesses for this case. It was only late last week that we were informed he would be available to testify."

"What about the 'no connection' charge? What is your response?"

"We expect Mr. Addison to identify the defendant as his primary assailant."

"Very well, then. Step back. Call Timothy Addison," he ordered.

"Your Honor," the defense attorney responded. "I renew my objection to this witness."

"Your objection is noted in the record. Now be seated."

There was a stir with audible murmuring, as witnesses, jury members, and spectators alike craned to get a view of the man who had been the unseen subject of these proceedings. The judge pounded his gavel demanding "order" again, trying to bring quiet back to the room.

"Please state your name," the bailiff instructed him after the attendants helped him from the wheelchair up into the witness box.

"Timothy Alan Addison."

"Please be seated Mr. Addison."

He sat down, searching for Mary's face in the crowd, hoping it would calm the rapid beating of his heart. Finding her smile, he relaxed a little, as the prosecutor approached the witness stand.

"Good Morning, Mr. Addison," Grant Hughes said, glancing covertly at the jury, looking for the expressions of sympathy he expected, hoping they were replaying his words of the previous week.

He couldn't know that in each mind simultaneously, those words replayed. "Ladies and gentlemen we will be asking you to deliver a vote of guilty and deliver justice for this young man who has been wrongly and maliciously injured by the evil wanton acts of the defendant and his, recently deceased partner-in-crime. What we want, since the victim is still suffering greatly and may be unable to appear in person, is for you to envision a long-awaited and carefully planned fishing and hiking adventure – the very type of outing that any one of you, your children or grandchildren could undertake – only to be abducted, robbed, terrorized, assaulted, beaten and left for dead by two good-for-nothing petty hoods looking for funding for their next round of beer and pot." He paused.

"Ladies and gentlemen of the jury," Hughes had said barely above a whisper, "It is up to you to tell these vermin who run loose in our society that we will no longer tolerate scavengers and parasites." His voice literally hissed as he delivered these last words.

Tim Addison became even more uncomfortable at the length of time the prosecutor left him sitting in the witness chair before he began his questioning. He was aware that a stage was being set, a scenario being painted, with his appearance at the center, but he was really not happy to be in this picture.

"Mr. Addison," Grant Hughes finally resumed turning his attention to the man in the witness chair. "You are not a resident of Colorado. Is that correct?"

Slightly annoyed by this beginning, since everyone there knew where he was from, Tim braced himself for a long ride. "No sir. I am from Richmond, Va."

"Would you explain to the court what brought you to Colorado last July?"

"I needed to get away from home for a while. So I decided to do some fishing in New Mexico and hiking in Colorado."

"Had you been to the area before?"

"Yes. Several times. I was a ski instructor in Aspen a couple of years back."

"At what point was your trip interrupted?"

"I was fishing near Chama, New Mexico. I think it was around the twenty-first of July."

"Would you tell the court exactly what happened?"

"I was approached by two men. They seemed friendly enough. One of them asked if I had caught anything? When I said no, they offered to show me some real fishing spots off the beaten path. I said sure, I was eager to find some fish. So, I gathered up my gear and headed for my Bronco, when one of the guys suggested that they ride with me, to make sure I didn't get lost. I became a little suspicious, but I figured I was just over-reacting. So we all got in my truck and drove off deep into the back woods, twisting here and turning there till I thought we were going in circles. After about a half-hour, we arrived at a cabin not far from a really nice looking mountain stream. I figured this must be the place, so I asked, 'Is this it?' 'This'll do,' one of them said, which sounded strange. I parked the Bronco and went over to have a look at the stream, watching the two of them out of the corner of my eye. They seemed to be arguing about something."

"What happened next, Mr. Addison?"

"They came back toward me as I was going through my gear. One of them was holding a gun. I asked them what the deal was."

"Mr. Addison, I'd like you to take a look at this picture. Do you recognize this person as one of the two men?"

"Yes. That's one of them."

"Your honor," Grant Hughes said as he approached the bench offering the photo to the Judge. "Let the record show that Mr. Addison has positively identified William Whaley, deceased, as one of his assailants."

"The record will so indicate," the Judge stated taking the picture then handing it to the court clerk.

"Now, Mr. Addison," the prosecutor said returning to the stand. "Can you tell us the identity of the other man in the party?"

"Yes, I can."

"Is he in this courtroom?"

"Yes, he is."

"Would you indicate the person?"

"It is the defendant, Mr. Baldwin."

First a whisper then a roar occurred in the courtroom.

"Order!" the Judge demanded, pounding his gavel.

"Now Mr. Addison, I realize this may be difficult for you, but would you please tell the court exactly what transpired after the two men abducted you."

"Well. First they took me into the cabin where they bound my hands and legs with duct tape and stuffed a filthy rag in my mouth. Then, they took my wallet, my credit cards and all the money that I had with me."

"How much money did you have?"

"About four hundred dollars. Maybe a little more."

Tim paused, seeming to reflect on the details of that day. His head was surprisingly clear, he realized. He looked at Mary, sitting next to his brother Mark. Then his eyes met those of Baldwin. The evil look in the man's eyes made his blood run cold.

"Please go on, Mr. Addison. Take your time, but we need to know everything that happened."

"They tied me to a chair and left. I don't know exactly how long they were gone – probably just till late the next day, though it seemed much longer. While they were gone, I tried to free myself, but the tape was too tight."

"So, Mr. Addison, for at least a period of twenty-four hours you were bound and gagged?"

"Yes. That's correct."

"No food?"

"No sir."

"No water?" he asked as he stared at the jury, hoping they were getting the full impact of these answers.

"No sir. "

"No bathroom?" he concluded moving back to the witness chair.

Tim dropped his head in embarrassment recalling the indignity of the situation.

"Mr. Addison," Grant Hughes prompted, "Did you have the use of any bathroom facilities?"

"No," he responded without looking up.

"Please tell the court what happened when the two men came back."

After a pause, Tim raised his head having regained control with the aid of something new to focus on and began speaking again very slowly.

"They were arguing. They seemed angry at each other about something that had happened while they were gone. Baldwin yelled at Whaley, something like, 'now they know. Now we have no choice. You jackass,' then he struck Whaley."

"Go on."

"Then, Baldwin came over to me – still in a rage. I guess I thought he was going to hit me next. But he cut the tape which bound me to the chair. I thought he was going to cut me free. Instead, after that, he just threw me across his shoulder, like a sack of flour or something. Outside, he put me on the back seat of the Bronco. They got in the front. They were still arguing. Whaley asked, 'why don't we just do it here and then be gone?' Baldwin glared at him and said very slowly – '…because, moron. This is my cabin.' Then they drove away. I don't know how far we traveled – but it was well into the night when they stopped."

"Did they say anything to you or to each other as they drove along that night?"

"Not really. Baldwin looked back over the seat at me several times. He may have said something, I don't really recall." Tim dropped his head again, not really wanting to recall the words and the looks of his captor.

"What were you thinking, bound and gagged in the back of the vehicle like that? Were you scared? Did they do or say anything further to terrorize you?"

"They were both rather quiet for a long time. I stared out the window at all the stars. I remember wondering if I would ever see the night sky again. Then I prayed, not necessarily for deliverance. But, if I was going to die at the hands of these two men," Tim lifted his head, looking at Marvin Baldwin without flinching or feeling any further fear. "If they were going to take my life, I prayed for the strength to die with dignity. I did not want them to take my dignity and self respect."

The courtroom was quiet for what seemed a very long time as Tim Addison held the stare of Marvin Baldwin. Then something very strange occurred. He smiled at his assailant and said, almost to himself, "I won."

With that, jurors and spectators throughout the room looked at each other questioningly. More than one person was heard to ask, "What did he say?"

Grant Hughes turned back to Tim, "Mr. Addison, what happened after they stopped the vehicle."

"I'm not sure. I just remember being struck several times with an object before I was hit on the head. The next thing I know, I'm in a hospital bed in Richmond, about a month later."

"Thank you Mr. Addison," Hughes said turning away from the stand. "Your witness, counselor."

At first the defense attorney seemed at a loss. Then he asked, "Your honor, we request a ten minute recess to confer with my client."

The judge looked at his watch then spoke, "Since it is after eleven, court will recess for lunch and will resume at two o'clock."

TEN

Stewart Phillips the Public Defender assigned to defend Marvin Baldwin could be seen through the glass-partitioned room staring down at his client. His arms were waving in exaggerated gestures as he stood opposite the accused man.

"What do you suppose that's all about," Mark Addison wondered aloud.

"Probably reading him the riot act for not telling him the truth, would be my guess," Mary responded as they passed. Tim Addison sat silently in the wheelchair, amazed at the feeling of calm which had remained.

"I'm hungry," he spoke up to the surprise of the other two.

"Then let us be about finding food," his brother responded with a smile and a pat on the back.

The bright noon-day Colorado sun welcomed and warmed them all as they emerged from the dark courthouse. Spontaneous chatter, almost banter, in expression of relief that the ordeal was almost over was exchanged as they strolled down the avenue toward the small downtown diner on the corner.

"I want to go home," Tim said after they had ordered their food.

"We will. Very soon," his brother replied.

"No. I want to go home today," Tim insisted.

"Don't you want to stay for the finale," Mary questioned?

"No. I want to get as far away from this as I can. I want to get on with my life. If that's even possible, that is."

"Well," Mark ventured. "I suppose there is no real reason for you to remain."

"We probably should discuss it with Hughes," Mary suggested.

"I don't want to discuss it with anyone. I'm tired and I want to leave."

No further discussion of the matter ensued. Mary and Tim boarded the next available flight out of Denver for Dulles International and made connections back to Richmond. Mark Addison remained in Denver to explain the disappearance of the witness who had not been excused and to await the outcome of the trial.

ELEVEN

Tim Addison's further testimony was not required. When court re-convened, as the absence of the witness was being explained to the judge, Stew Phillips rose from his seat.

"Your honor, if it please the court, the Defense has no questions for Mr. Addison."

"Then let the record show," the judge began, "that the witness is excused from proceedings in absentia."

"Your honor," Phillips resumed, "request permission to approach with the Prosecutor."

"Approach," the judge responded.

"What's going on?" Judge Henry wanted to know.

"Your honor, my client wishes me to discuss the possibility of a plea bargain with Mr. Hughes. I tried unsuccessfully to locate the Prosecutor during the lunch recess. If your Honor has no objection, a thirty minute recess should be sufficient."

"Stand back," the judge responded. "This court is recessed for thirty minutes."

Hughes followed Phillips into the glass partitioned room where he had two hours earlier met with his client.

"I am tired of your lies and bullshit," he had yelled at Marvin Baldwin. "You are going to prison for a very long time. Let me tell you what I saw in the reaction on the faces on that jury to what you and your partner did to that kid. If they could do it, you would be on your way to death row. They want to string you up. And, quite frankly, I don't blame them. My only recommendation to you is that we plead guilty and see what kind of deal I can work out as far a reduced sentencing. I may already be too late. They have two more witnesses scheduled and I've got nothing. I haven't come up with even one person who will step forward and make any kind of statement on your behalf. Frankly, you deserve whatever you get. But, I would not be doing my job, at this point if I just sat and waited for the jury verdict – which is what I really would prefer to do."

Baldwin sat silently through the entire speech then rose, sneered at Phillips and said, "Go to Hell! Do whatever you want to do."

TWELVE

"I'm listening," Grant Hughes said after Phillips closed the door.

"My client is agreeable to pleading guilty to the charges of abduction, robbery and assault. However, he insists it was Whaley who hit Mr. Addison in the head. Since he can't remember or didn't even know which one hit him, I don't think you can make the attempted murder charge stick."

"You're out of your mind. That jury is going to give me whatever I ask for. You saw the looks on their faces. They were ready to form a lynch mob when Tim Addison finished his story."

"Look. I know you have a sympathetic victim and that the jury is convinced. I also know that Marvin Baldwin does not help our defense. I just want to get this thing finished without the jury's emotions coming in to play. I don't ever want to see this guy again. And I don't want some high-emotion jury verdict to give anyone a basis for appeal."

"What sort of sentence are you looking for?"

"Personally or as his attorney?"

"As his attorney."

"How does twenty years sound?"

"Not very appealing. With good behavior, he's out in five."

"Good behavior. This guy? He'll be lucky if someone doesn't kill him the first month he's in."

"Tell you what I'll do. Ten years each offense, served consecutively."

"Fine. Let's go talk to the judge."

THIRTEEN

The United Air flight touched down at Richmond's Byrd International just before nine o'clock. Tim had spoken fewer than a dozen words during both the flight from Denver and from Dulles. He was extremely tired and slept most of the time. When he wasn't asleep, he did not open his eyes.

As they walked through the terminal toward the baggage claim, Mary took his arm and steered him to a deserted waiting area.

"What is it?" he asked.

"I'm not sure. I know this has been a trying if not totally demoralizing experience to have to relive those events. But, it won't help if you just shut down and lock out the rest of the world, me included. I can only imagine the horror that you must have endured. But, I want to be here for you now. It's over. It's behind you."

"Is it? Will it really ever be over? Will there ever come a time when I close my eyes and that sneering ugly face will not be there? I doubt it."

"With the proper help and time, it will. I know it will."

"How do you know?"

"I just know. Trust me on this. I will help you get through this."

"I'm not sure I want to put you through this personal Hell of mine. I'm not sure I can ask you to do that – to share this with me."

"I don't see any other option. You have turned my life upside down, too. I was a missing person myself, just as surely and certainly as you were. Now we've found each other. Let's not lose that."

He squeezed her hand as he had when he first looked into those eyes, that beautiful face. Feeling confident for the first time that he could, with her beside him, battle and survive what ever troubles and torturous nights lay ahead.

"Hi," he said with a smile. "My name's Tim. But I guess you already knew that."

THE END